E Dun
Dunn, Joeming W.
The time machine

— H.G. Wells's —

The Time Machine

Adapted by
Joeming Dunn

Illustrated by
Ben Dunn

magic
wagon

visit us at
www.abdopublishing.com

Published by Magic Wagon, a division of the ABDO Publishing Group, 8000 West 78th Street, Edina, Minnesota 55439.

Printed in the United States.

Original novel by H.G. Wells
Adapted by Joeming Dunn
Illustrated by Ben Dunn
Colored by Joseph Wight and Robby Bevard
Lettered by Joeming Dunn
Edited by Stephanie Hedlund
Interior layout and design by Antarctic Press
Cover art by Ben Dunn
Cover design by Neil Klinepier

Library of Congress Cataloging-in-Publication Data

Dunn, Joeming W.
The Time Machine / H.G. Wells ; adapted by Joeming Dunn ; illustrated by Ben Dunn.
p. cm. -- (Graphic classics)
Includes bibliographical references.
ISBN 978-1-60270-054-3
1. Graphic novels. I. Dunn, Ben. II. Wells, H.G. (Herbert George), 1866-1946. Time Machine.
III. Title.

PN6727.D89T56 2008
741.5'973--dc22

2007006447

TABLE of CONTENTS

Chapter 1 Meeting the Time Traveler

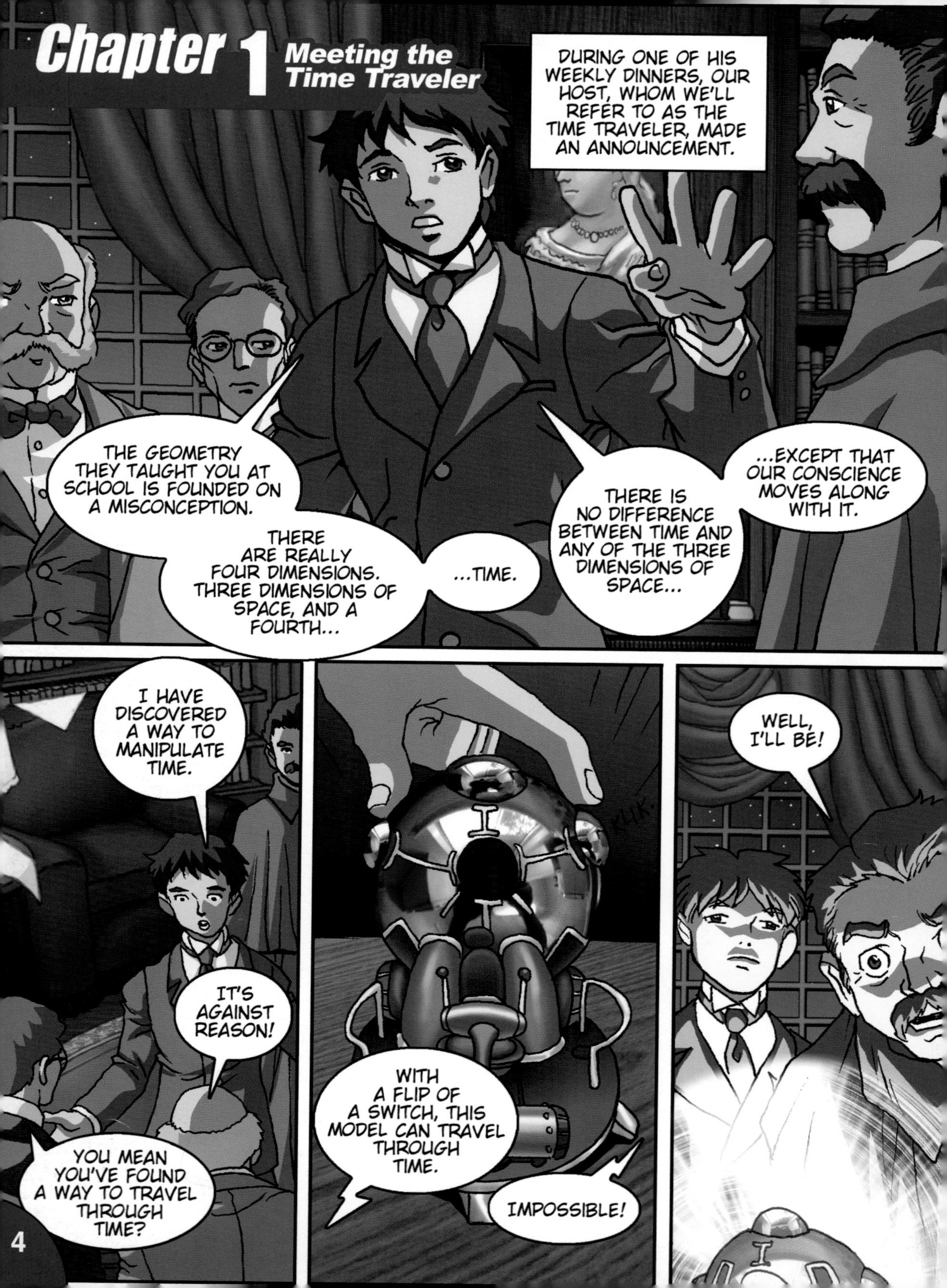
DURING ONE OF HIS WEEKLY DINNERS, OUR HOST, WHOM WE'LL REFER TO AS THE TIME TRAVELER, MADE AN ANNOUNCEMENT.
THE GEOMETRY THEY TAUGHT YOU AT SCHOOL IS FOUNDED ON A MISCONCEPTION.
THERE ARE REALLY FOUR DIMENSIONS. THREE DIMENSIONS OF SPACE, AND A FOURTH...
...TIME.
THERE IS NO DIFFERENCE BETWEEN TIME AND ANY OF THE THREE DIMENSIONS OF SPACE...
...EXCEPT THAT OUR CONSCIENCE MOVES ALONG WITH IT.
I HAVE DISCOVERED A WAY TO MANIPULATE TIME.
IT'S AGAINST REASON!
YOU MEAN YOU'VE FOUND A WAY TO TRAVEL THROUGH TIME?
KLIK.
WITH A FLIP OF A SWITCH, THIS MODEL CAN TRAVEL THROUGH TIME.
IMPOSSIBLE!
WELL, I'LL BE!

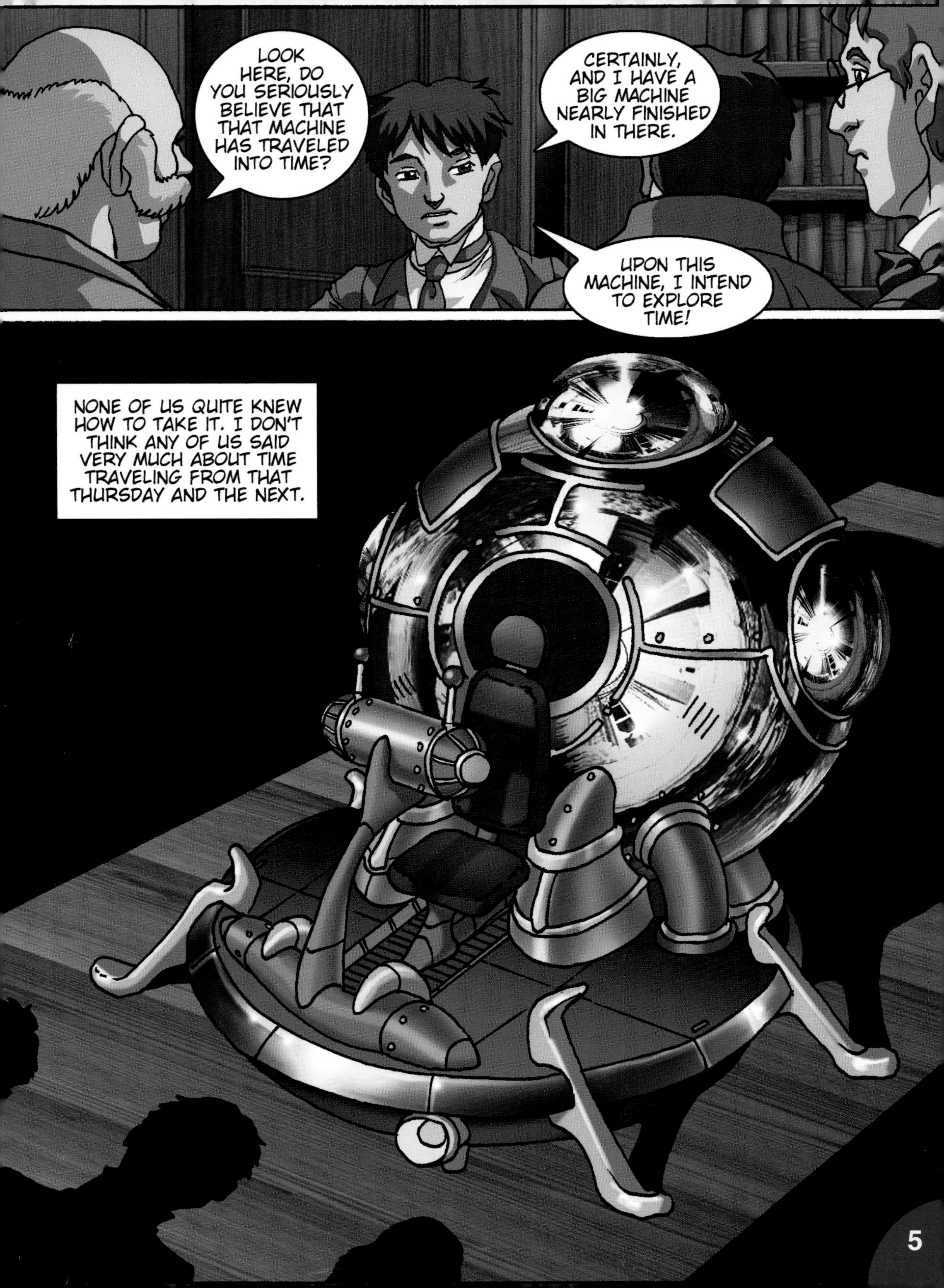
LOOK HERE, DO YOU SERIOUSLY BELIEVE THAT THAT MACHINE HAS TRAVELED INTO TIME?
CERTAINLY, AND I HAVE A BIG MACHINE NEARLY FINISHED IN THERE.
UPON THIS MACHINE, I INTEND TO EXPLORE TIME!
NONE OF US QUITE KNEW HOW TO TAKE IT. I DON'T THINK ANY OF US SAID VERY MUCH ABOUT TIME TRAVELING FROM THAT THURSDAY AND THE NEXT.

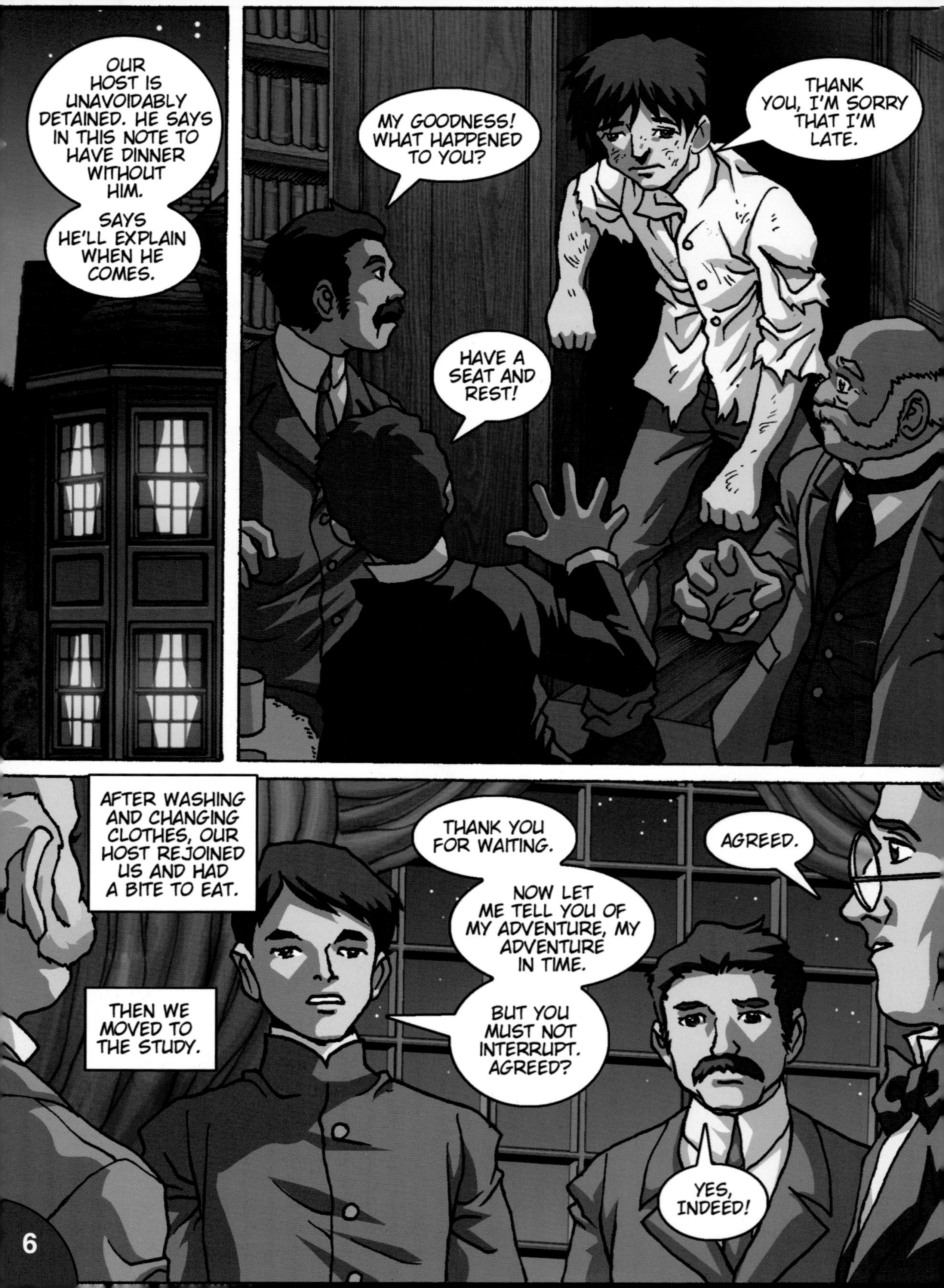
OUR HOST IS UNAVOIDABLY DETAINED. HE SAYS IN THIS NOTE TO HAVE DINNER WITHOUT HIM.
SAYS HE'LL EXPLAIN WHEN HE COMES.
MY GOODNESS! WHAT HAPPENED TO YOU?
THANK YOU, I'M SORRY THAT I'M LATE.
HAVE A SEAT AND REST!
AFTER WASHING AND CHANGING CLOTHES, OUR HOST REJOINED US AND HAD A BITE TO EAT.
THEN WE MOVED TO THE STUDY.
THANK YOU FOR WAITING.
NOW LET ME TELL YOU OF MY ADVENTURE, MY ADVENTURE IN TIME.
BUT YOU MUST NOT INTERRUPT. AGREED?
AGREED.
YES, INDEED!

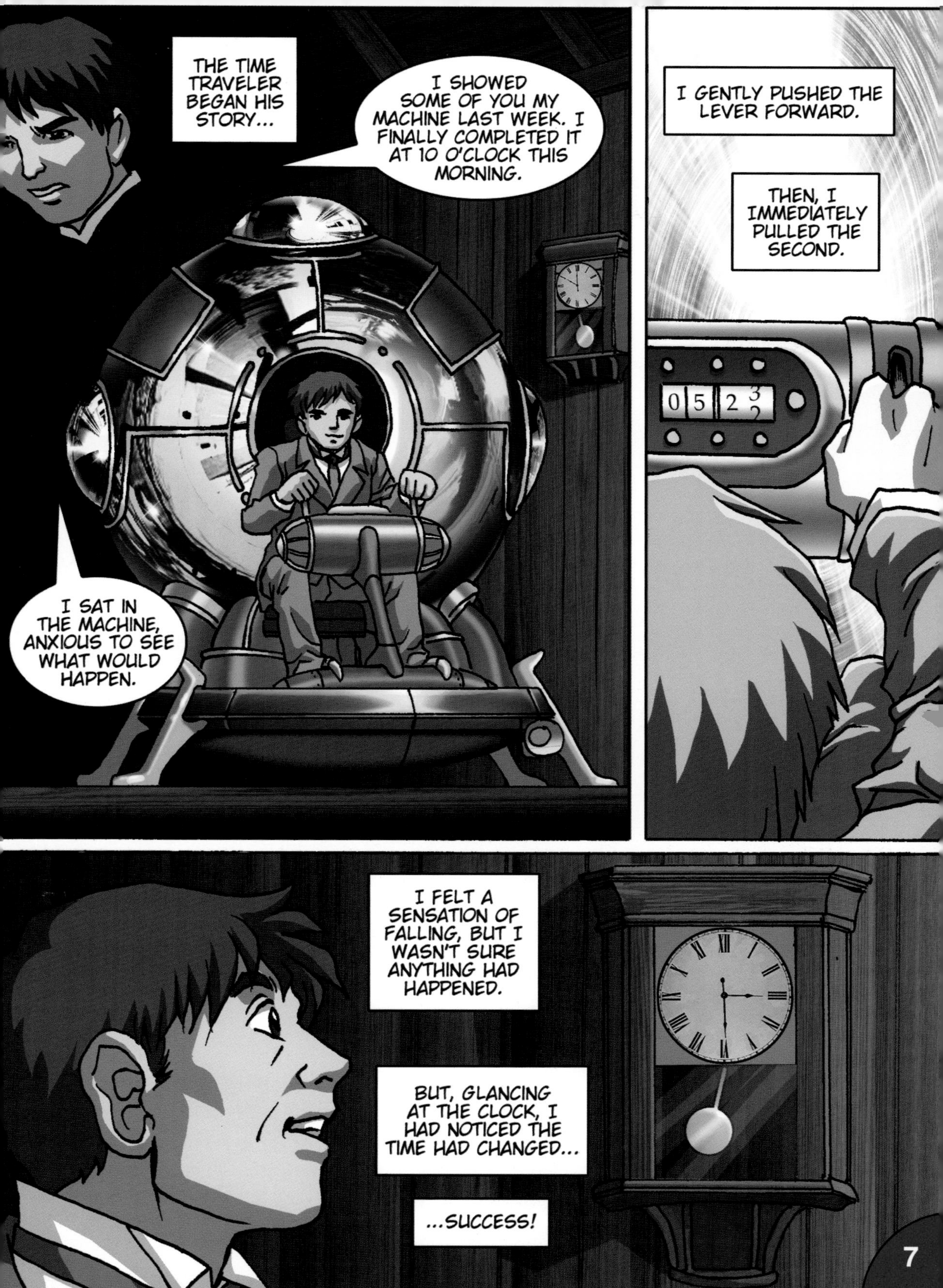
THE TIME TRAVELER BEGAN HIS STORY...
I SHOWED SOME OF YOU MY MACHINE LAST WEEK. I FINALLY COMPLETED IT AT 10 O'CLOCK THIS MORNING.
I SAT IN THE MACHINE, ANXIOUS TO SEE WHAT WOULD HAPPEN.
I GENTLY PUSHED THE LEVER FORWARD.
THEN, I IMMEDIATELY PULLED THE SECOND.
I FELT A SENSATION OF FALLING, BUT I WASN'T SURE ANYTHING HAD HAPPENED.
BUT, GLANCING AT THE CLOCK, I HAD NOTICED THE TIME HAD CHANGED...
...SUCCESS!

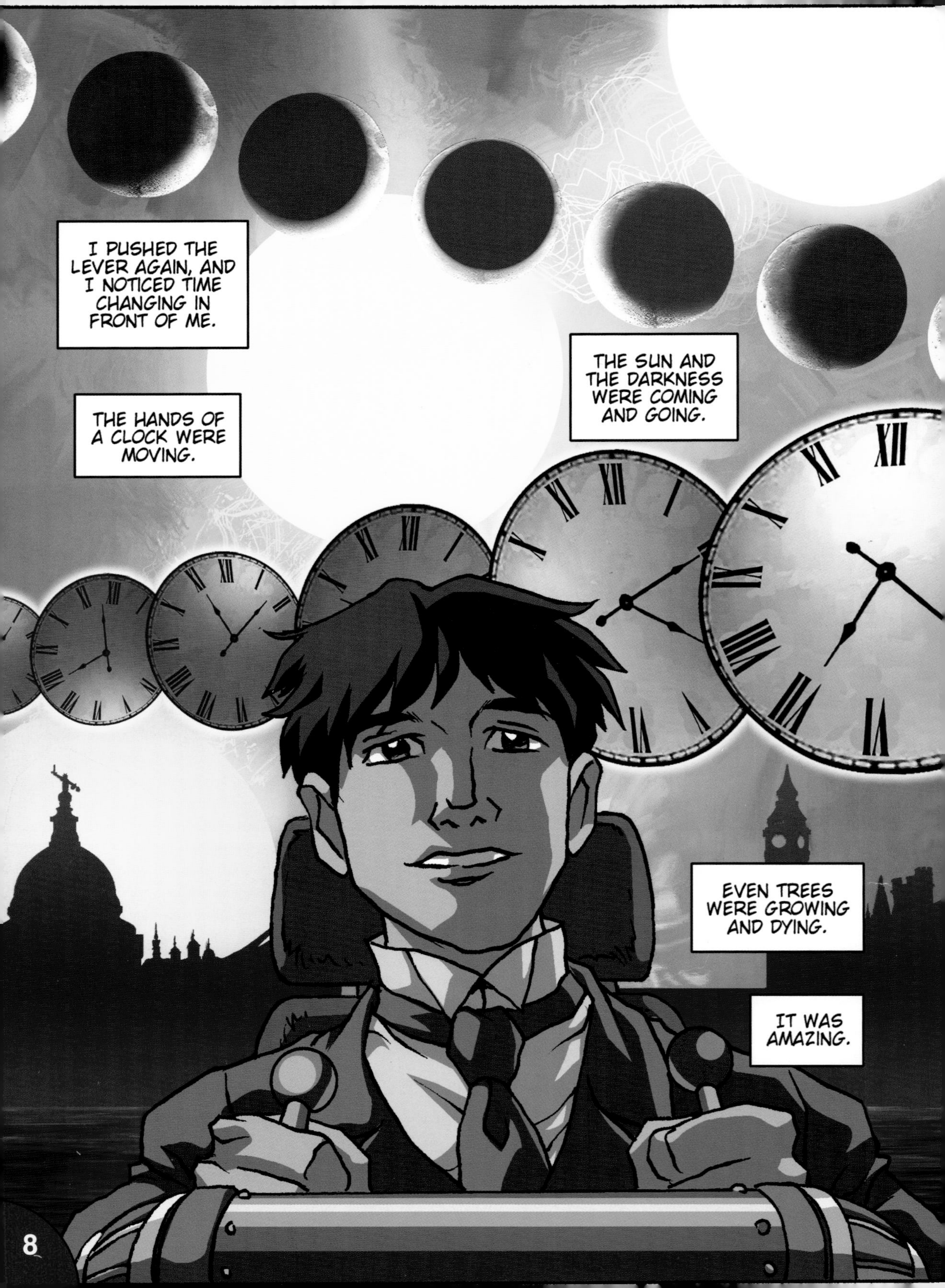
I PUSHED THE LEVER AGAIN, AND I NOTICED TIME CHANGING IN FRONT OF ME.
THE HANDS OF A CLOCK WERE MOVING.
THE SUN AND THE DARKNESS WERE COMING AND GOING.
EVEN TREES WERE GROWING AND DYING.
IT WAS AMAZING.

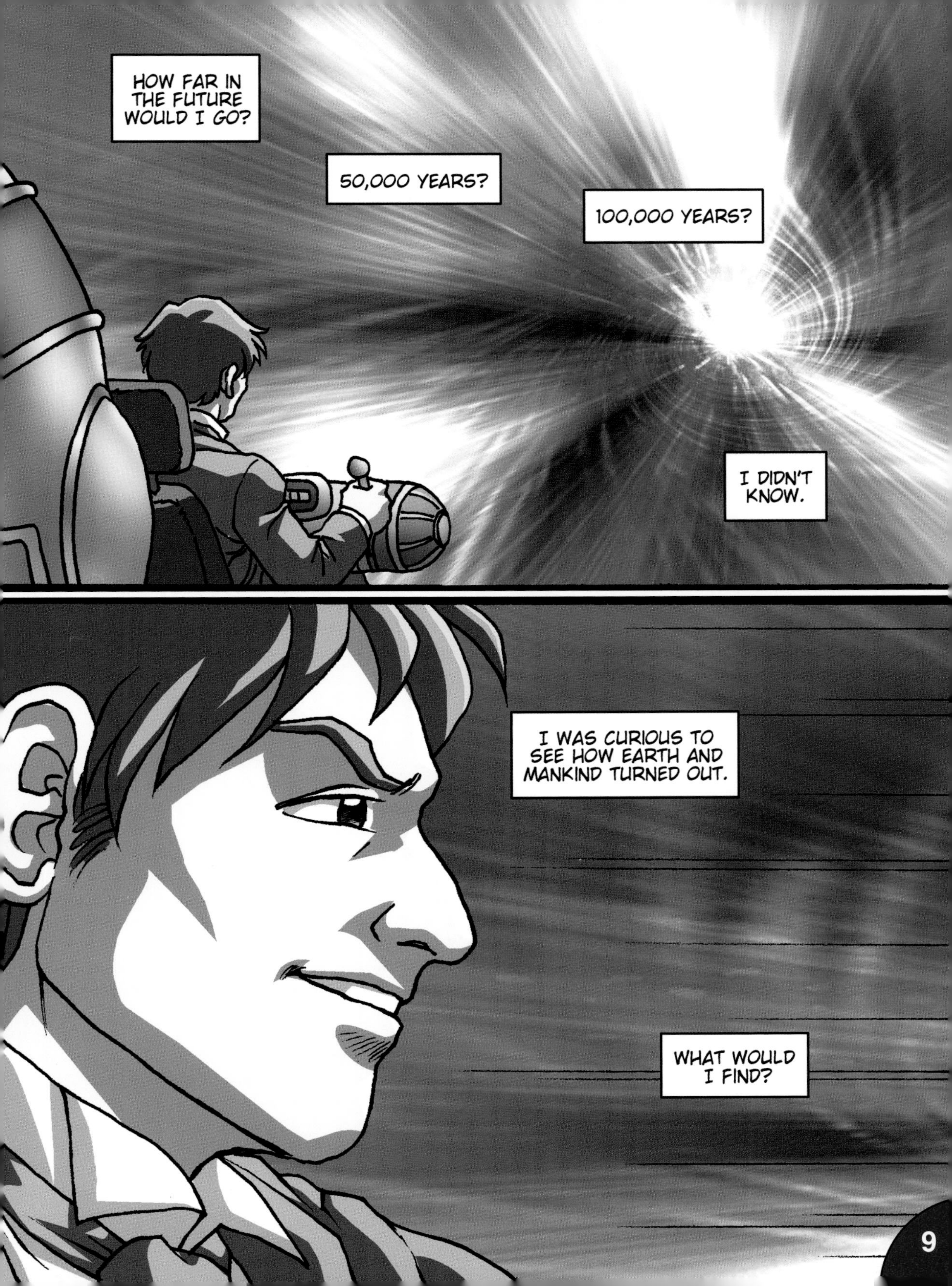
HOW FAR IN THE FUTURE WOULD I GO?
50,000 YEARS?
100,000 YEARS?
I DIDN'T KNOW.
I WAS CURIOUS TO SEE HOW EARTH AND MANKIND TURNED OUT.
WHAT WOULD I FIND?

Chapter 2 The Eloi

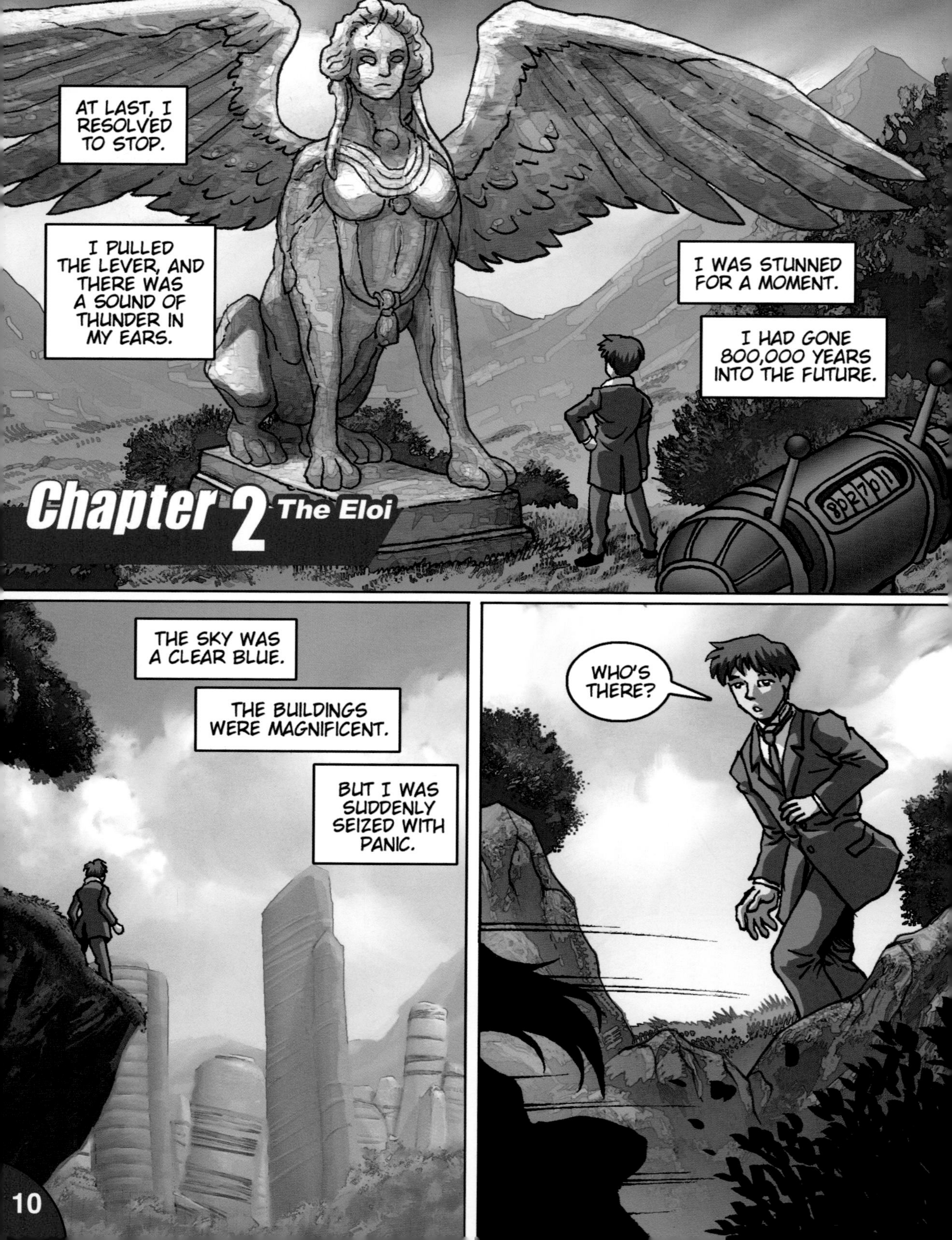
AT LAST, I RESOLVED TO STOP.
I PULLED THE LEVER, AND THERE WAS A SOUND OF THUNDER IN MY EARS.
I WAS STUNNED FOR A MOMENT.
I HAD GONE 800,000 YEARS INTO THE FUTURE.
THE SKY WAS A CLEAR BLUE.
THE BUILDINGS WERE MAGNIFICENT.
BUT I WAS SUDDENLY SEIZED WITH PANIC.
WHO'S THERE?

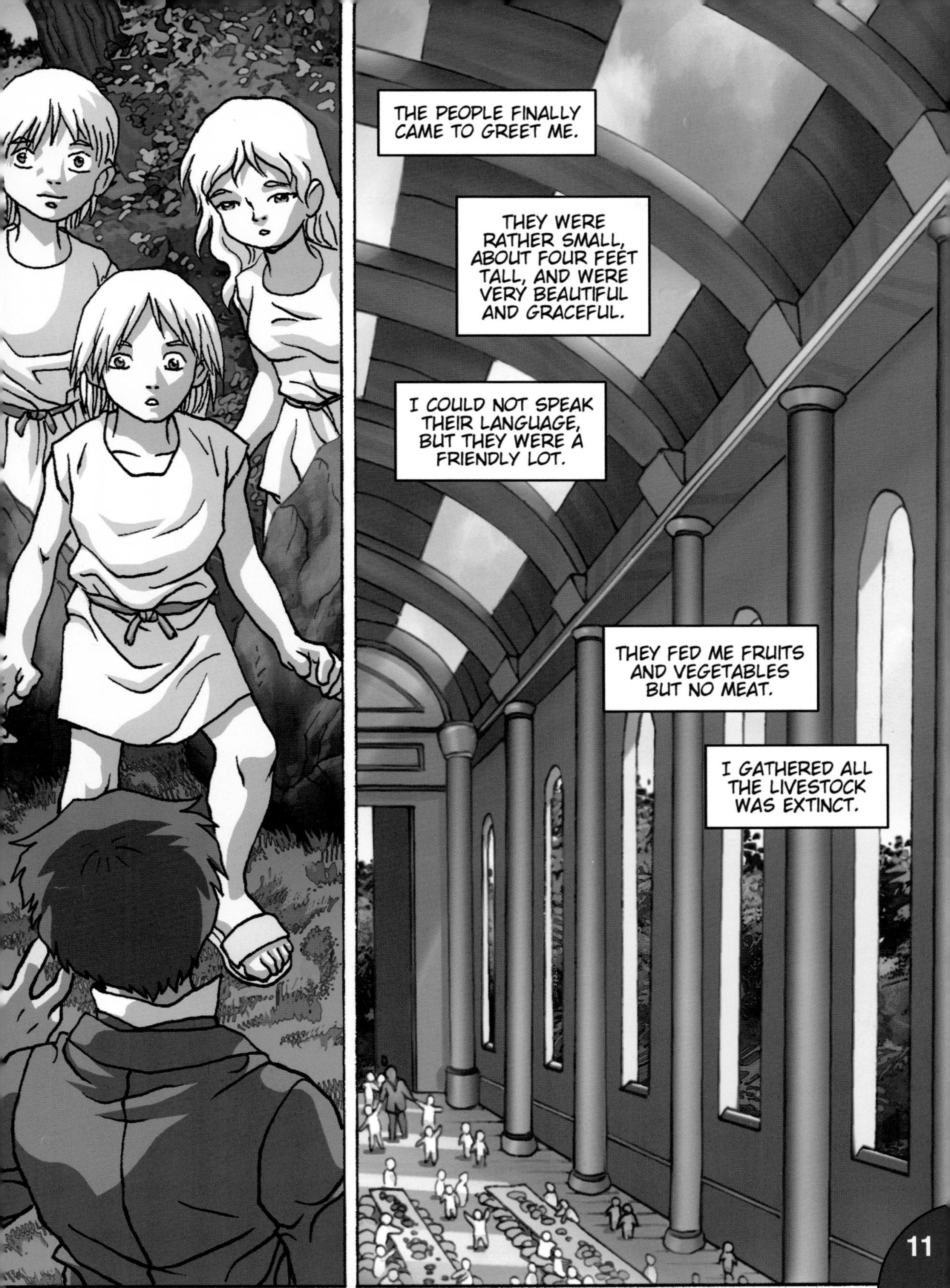
THE PEOPLE FINALLY CAME TO GREET ME.
THEY WERE RATHER SMALL, ABOUT FOUR FEET TALL, AND WERE VERY BEAUTIFUL AND GRACEFUL.
I COULD NOT SPEAK THEIR LANGUAGE, BUT THEY WERE A FRIENDLY LOT.
THEY FED ME FRUITS AND VEGETABLES BUT NO MEAT.
I GATHERED ALL THE LIVESTOCK WAS EXTINCT.

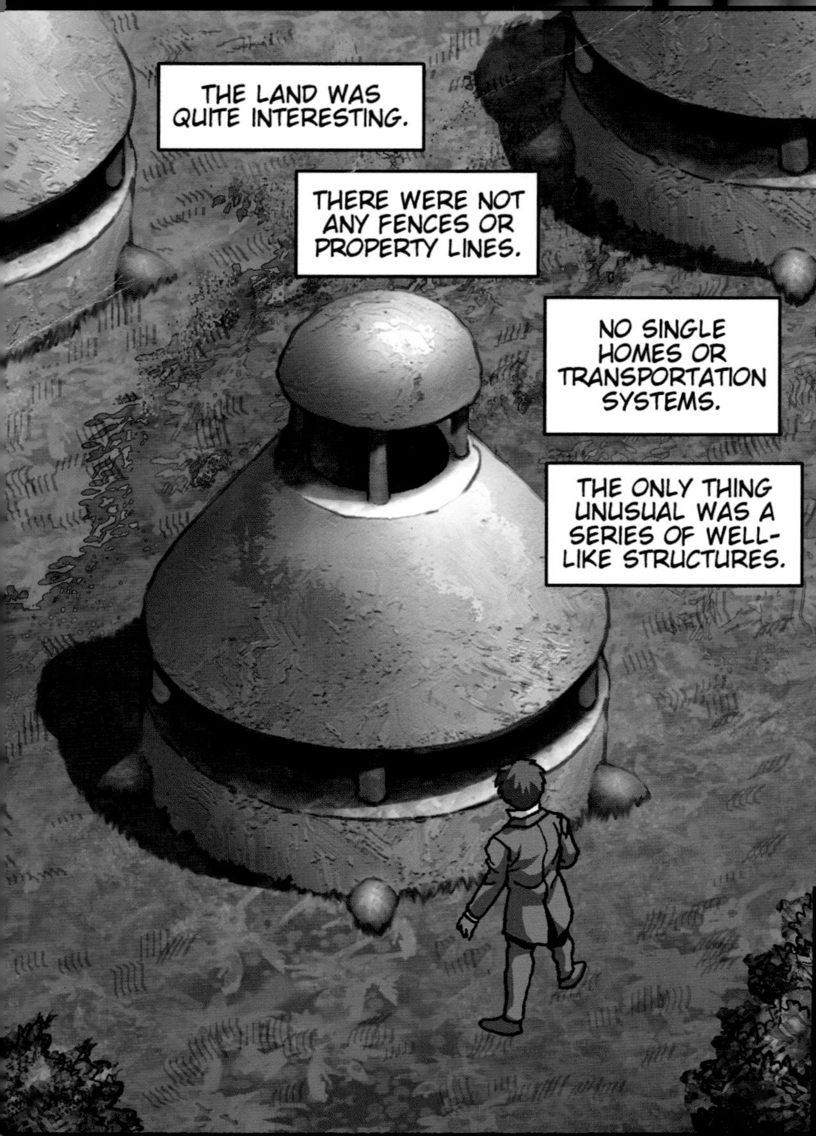
THE LAND WAS QUITE INTERESTING.
THERE WERE NOT ANY FENCES OR PROPERTY LINES.
NO SINGLE HOMES OR TRANSPORTATION SYSTEMS.
THE ONLY THING UNUSUAL WAS A SERIES OF WELL-LIKE STRUCTURES.

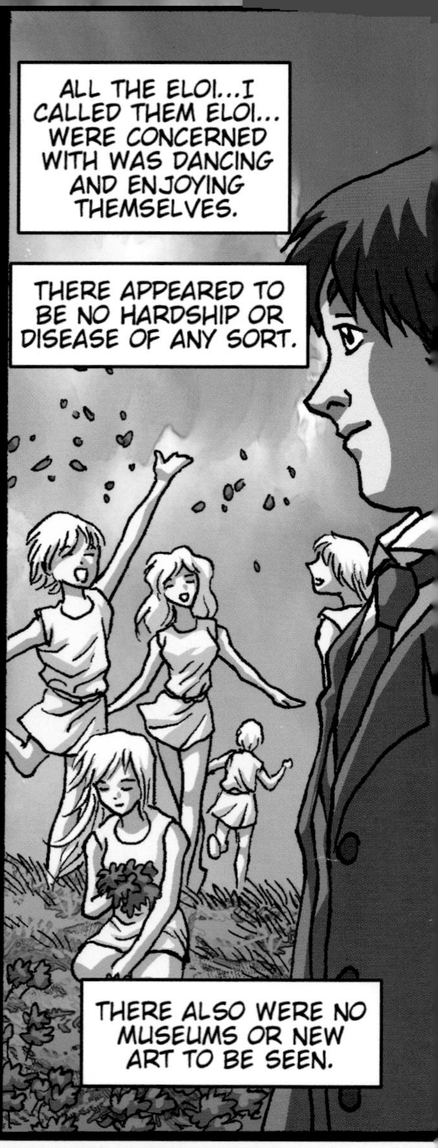
ALL THE ELOI...I CALLED THEM ELOI... WERE CONCERNED WITH WAS DANCING AND ENJOYING THEMSELVES.
THERE APPEARED TO BE NO HARDSHIP OR DISEASE OF ANY SORT.
THERE ALSO WERE NO MUSEUMS OR NEW ART TO BE SEEN.

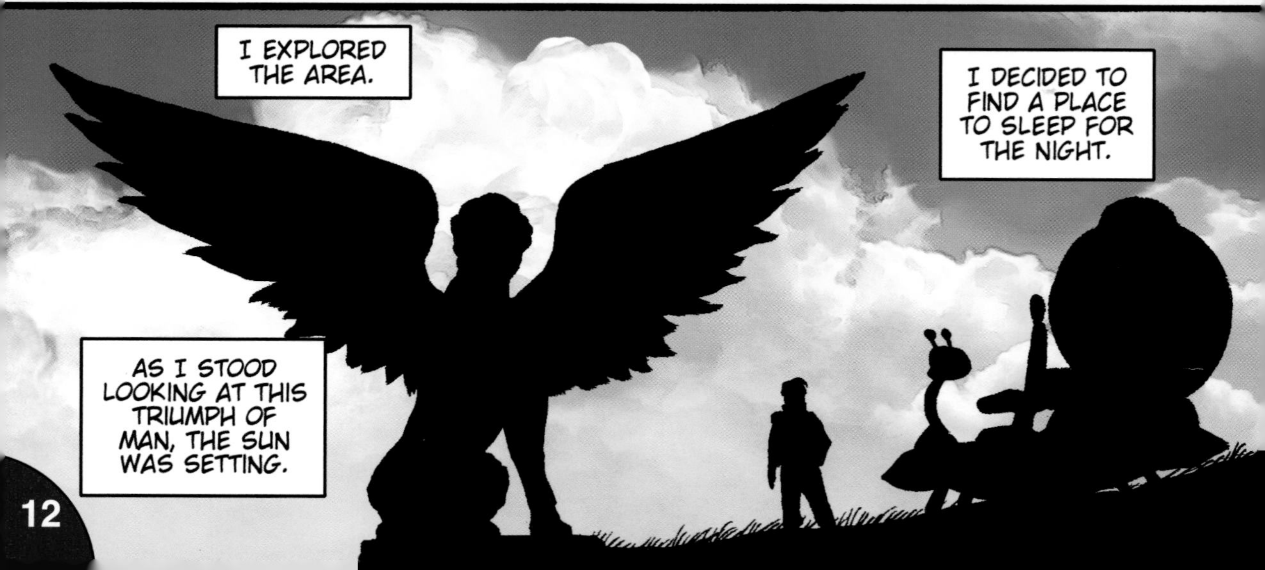
I EXPLORED THE AREA.
I DECIDED TO FIND A PLACE TO SLEEP FOR THE NIGHT.
AS I STOOD LOOKING AT THIS TRIUMPH OF MAN, THE SUN WAS SETTING.

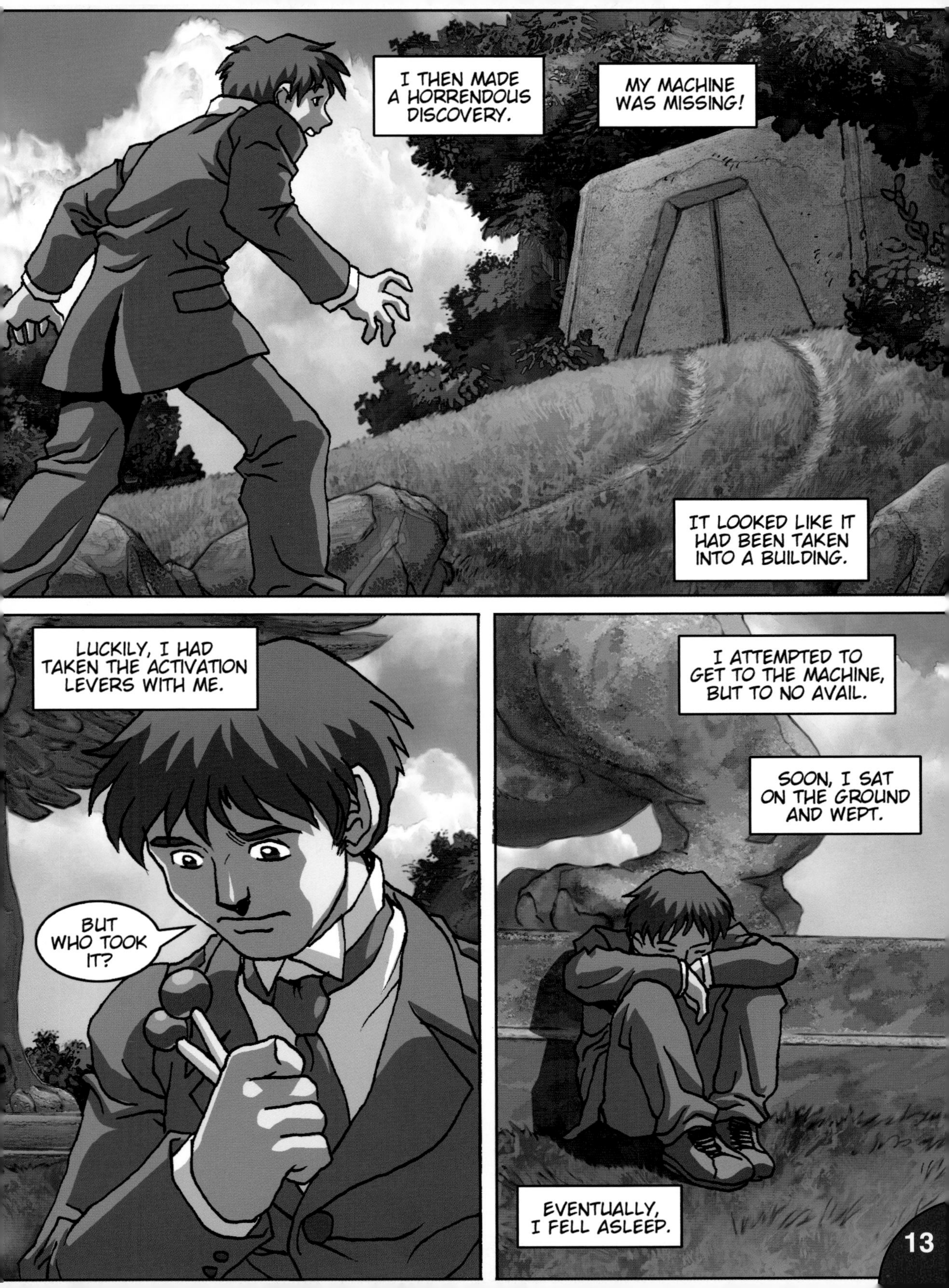
I THEN MADE A HORRENDOUS DISCOVERY.
MY MACHINE WAS MISSING!
IT LOOKED LIKE IT HAD BEEN TAKEN INTO A BUILDING.
LUCKILY, I HAD TAKEN THE ACTIVATION LEVERS WITH ME.
BUT WHO TOOK IT?
I ATTEMPTED TO GET TO THE MACHINE, BUT TO NO AVAIL.
SOON, I SAT ON THE GROUND AND WEPT.
EVENTUALLY, I FELL ASLEEP.

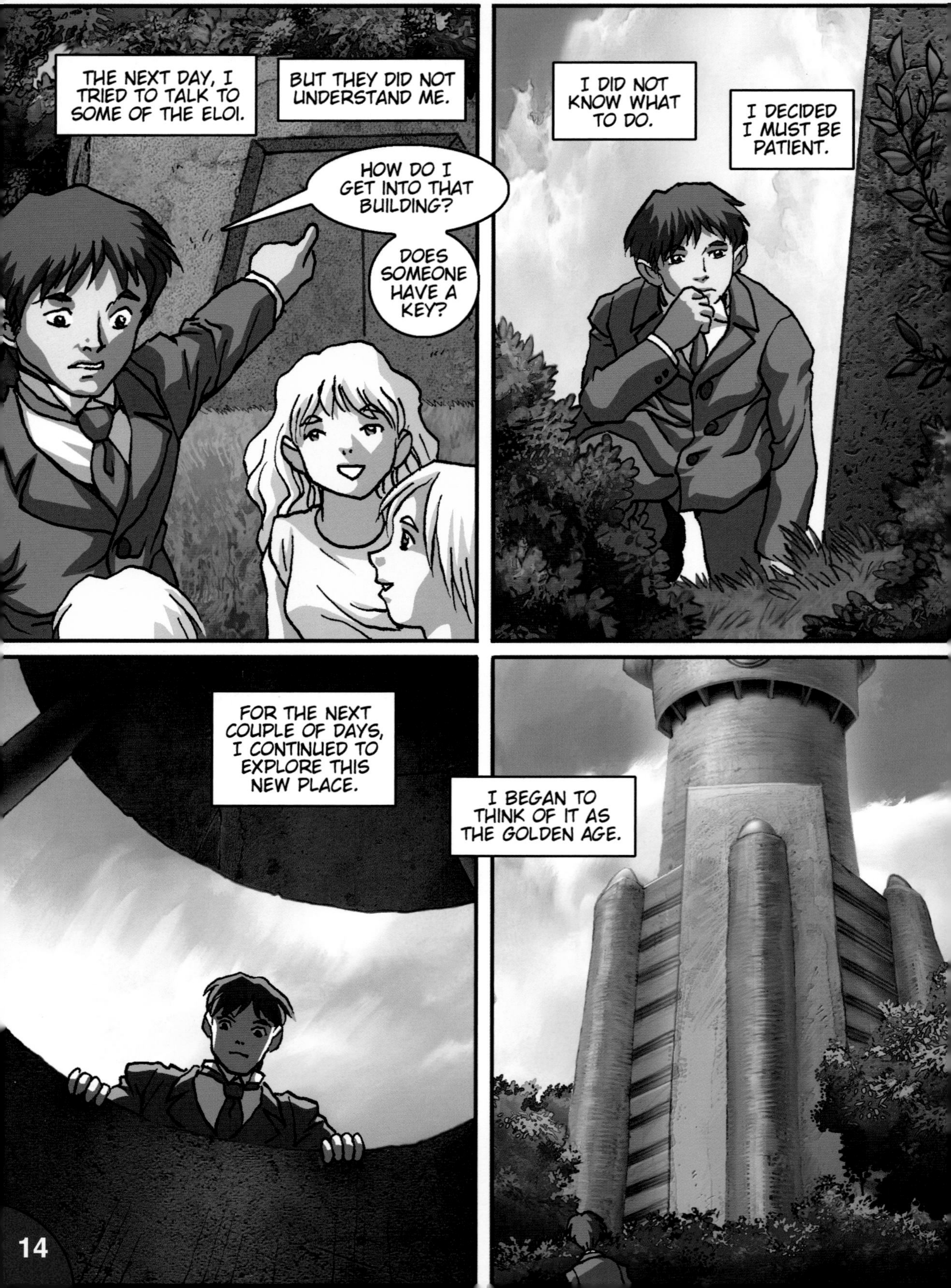
THE NEXT DAY, I TRIED TO TALK TO SOME OF THE ELOI.
BUT THEY DID NOT UNDERSTAND ME.
HOW DO I GET INTO THAT BUILDING?
DOES SOMEONE HAVE A KEY?
I DID NOT KNOW WHAT TO DO.
I DECIDED I MUST BE PATIENT.
FOR THE NEXT COUPLE OF DAYS, I CONTINUED TO EXPLORE THIS NEW PLACE.
I BEGAN TO THINK OF IT AS THE GOLDEN AGE.

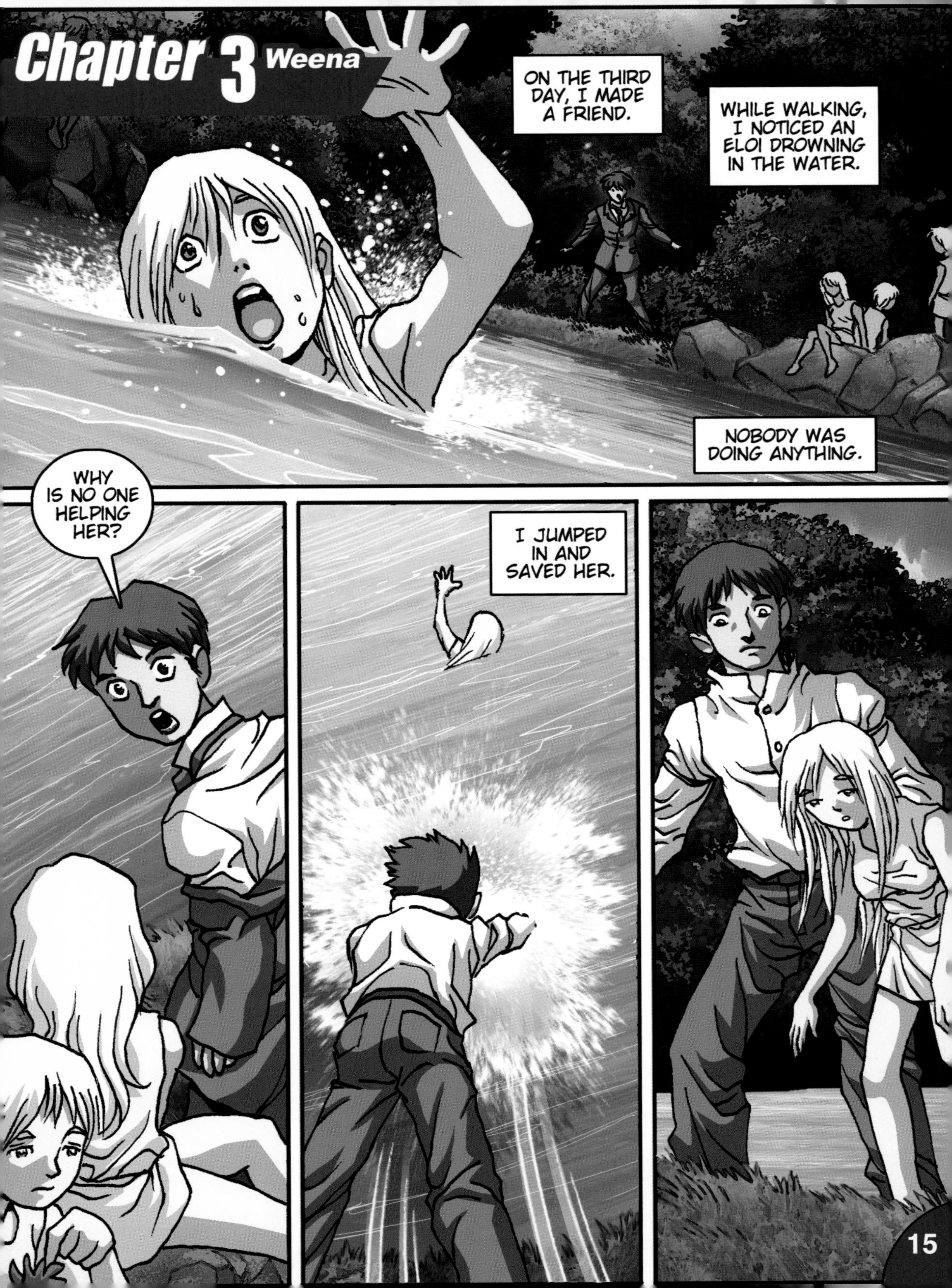
Chapter 3 Weena
ON THE THIRD DAY, I MADE A FRIEND.
WHILE WALKING, I NOTICED AN ELOI DROWNING IN THE WATER.
NOBODY WAS DOING ANYTHING.
WHY IS NO ONE HELPING HER?
I JUMPED IN AND SAVED HER.

THE WOMAN WAS VERY APPRECIATIVE OF MY HELP.

SHE PRESENTED ME A GIFT, A GARLAND.

WE SOON BECAME FRIENDS.

I LEARNED THAT HER NAME WAS WEENA.

AND I LEARNED SOME OF THE ELOI LANGUAGE FROM HER.

OH... THAT MEANS HANDS.

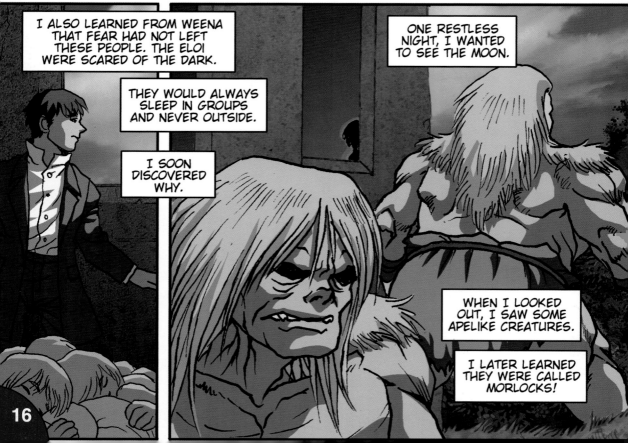

I ALSO LEARNED FROM WEENA THAT FEAR HAD NOT LEFT THESE PEOPLE. THE ELOI WERE SCARED OF THE DARK.

THEY WOULD ALWAYS SLEEP IN GROUPS AND NEVER OUTSIDE.

I SOON DISCOVERED WHY.

ONE RESTLESS NIGHT, I WANTED TO SEE THE MOON.

WHEN I LOOKED OUT, I SAW SOME APELIKE CREATURES.

I LATER LEARNED THEY WERE CALLED MORLOCKS!

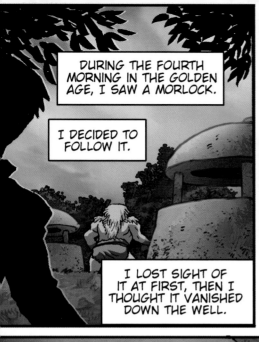

DURING THE FOURTH MORNING IN THE GOLDEN AGE, I SAW A MORLOCK.

I DECIDED TO FOLLOW IT.

I LOST SIGHT OF IT AT FIRST, THEN I THOUGHT IT VANISHED DOWN THE WELL.

THIS DISCOVERY WAS ASTONISHING. THERE HAD TO BE ANOTHER SPECIES LIVING UNDERGROUND.

NO!

I DECIDED THEY MUST HAVE TAKEN MY TIME MACHINE.

I WAS READY TO FOLLOW THE MORLOCKS INTO THE WELL.

WEENA TRIED TO STOP ME.

FORBIDDEN... NO!

I MUST GO!

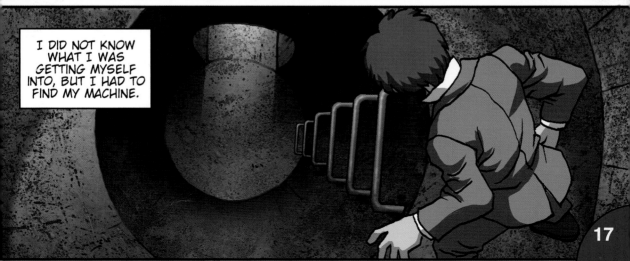

I DID NOT KNOW WHAT I WAS GETTING MYSELF INTO, BUT I HAD TO FIND MY MACHINE.

Chapter 4 The Morlock Lair

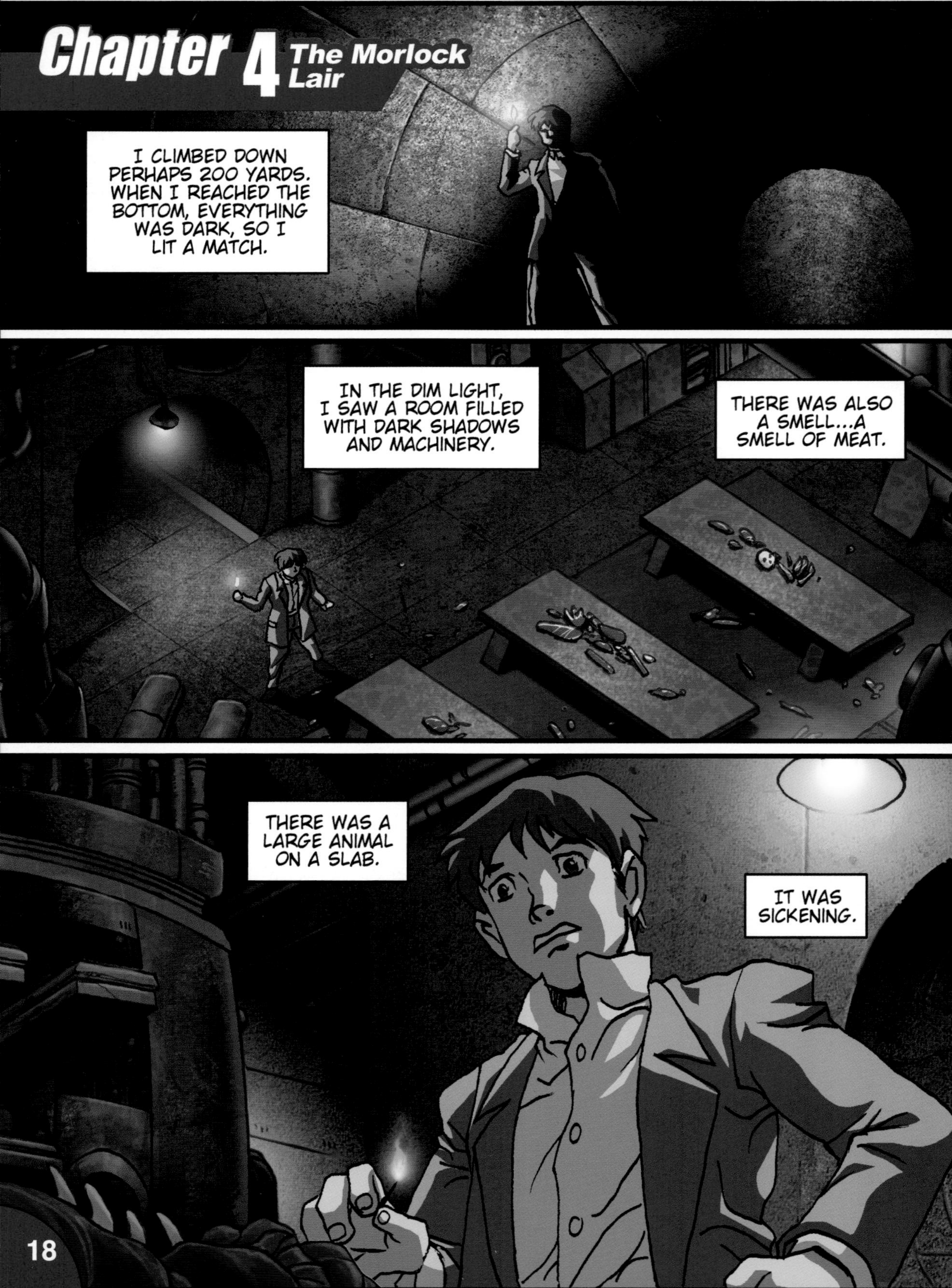
I CLIMBED DOWN PERHAPS 200 YARDS. WHEN I REACHED THE BOTTOM, EVERYTHING WAS DARK, SO I LIT A MATCH.
IN THE DIM LIGHT, I SAW A ROOM FILLED WITH DARK SHADOWS AND MACHINERY.
THERE WAS ALSO A SMELL...A SMELL OF MEAT.
THERE WAS A LARGE ANIMAL ON A SLAB.
IT WAS SICKENING.

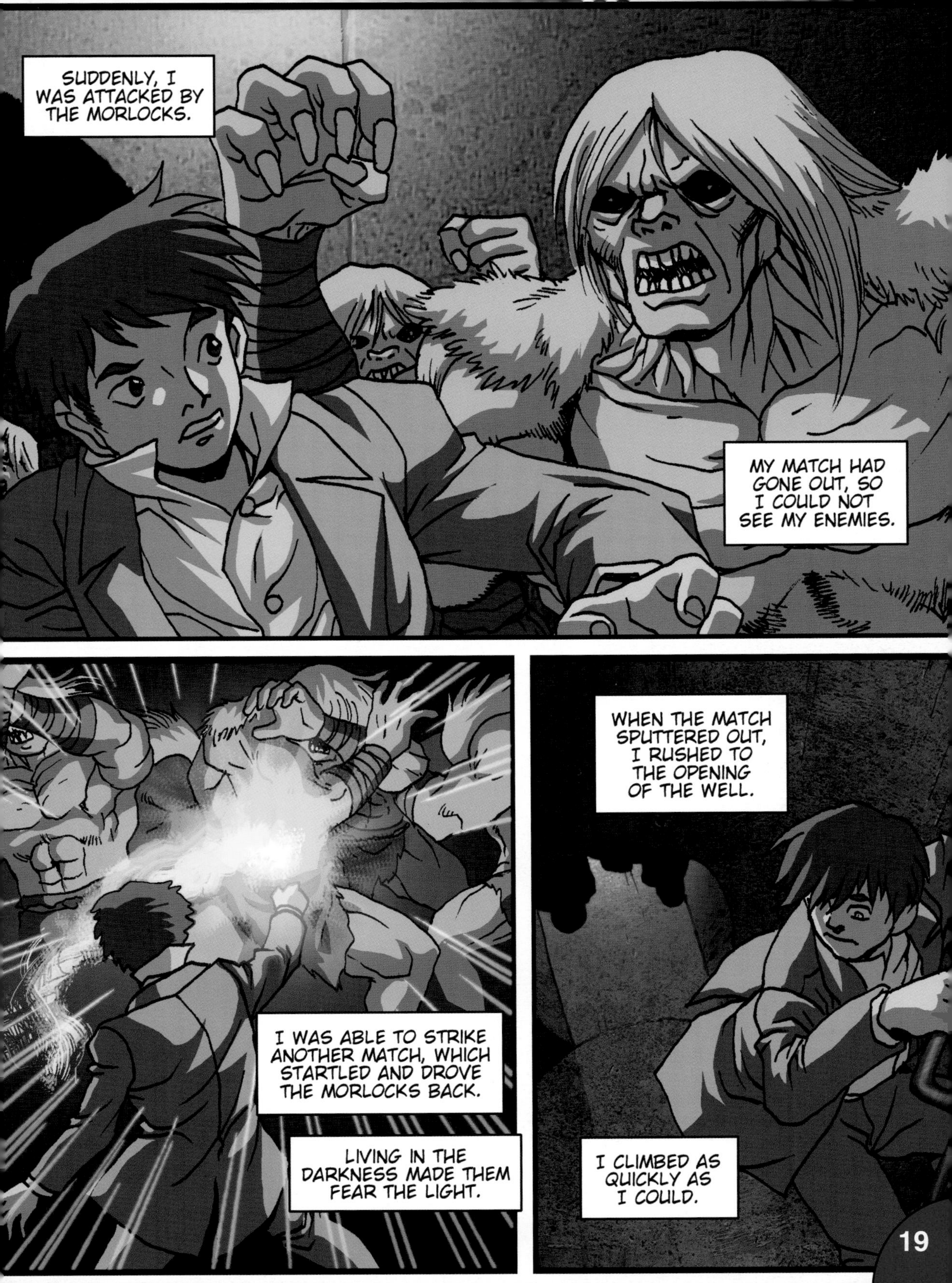
SUDDENLY, I WAS ATTACKED BY THE MORLOCKS.
MY MATCH HAD GONE OUT, SO I COULD NOT SEE MY ENEMIES.
I WAS ABLE TO STRIKE ANOTHER MATCH, WHICH STARTLED AND DROVE THE MORLOCKS BACK.
LIVING IN THE DARKNESS MADE THEM FEAR THE LIGHT.
WHEN THE MATCH SPUTTERED OUT, I RUSHED TO THE OPENING OF THE WELL.
I CLIMBED AS QUICKLY AS I COULD.

ONCE I REACHED SAFETY, I REVIEWED WHAT I HAD LEARNED.

I REALIZED THE MORLOCKS PROVIDED EVERYTHING FOR THE ELOI.

IN RETURN, THEY USED THE ELOI AS FOOD.

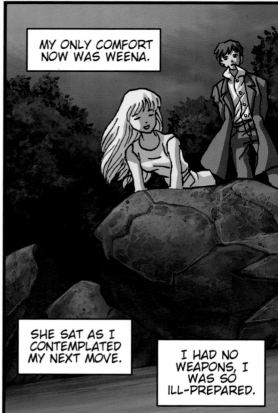

MY ONLY COMFORT NOW WAS WEENA.

SHE SAT AS I CONTEMPLATED MY NEXT MOVE.

I HAD NO WEAPONS, I WAS SO ILL-PREPARED.

SENSING MY DISTRESS, WEENA GAVE ME TWO FLOWERS.

IT WAS ALL THAT SHE COULD GIVE ME.

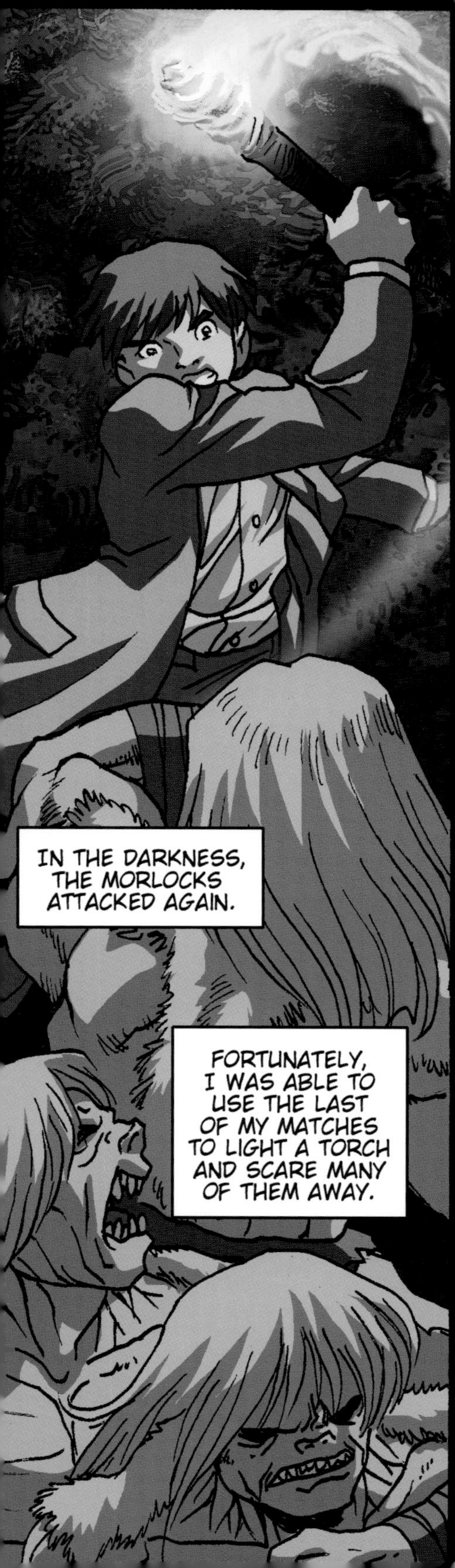
IN THE DARKNESS, THE MORLOCKS ATTACKED AGAIN.
FORTUNATELY, I WAS ABLE TO USE THE LAST OF MY MATCHES TO LIGHT A TORCH AND SCARE MANY OF THEM AWAY.

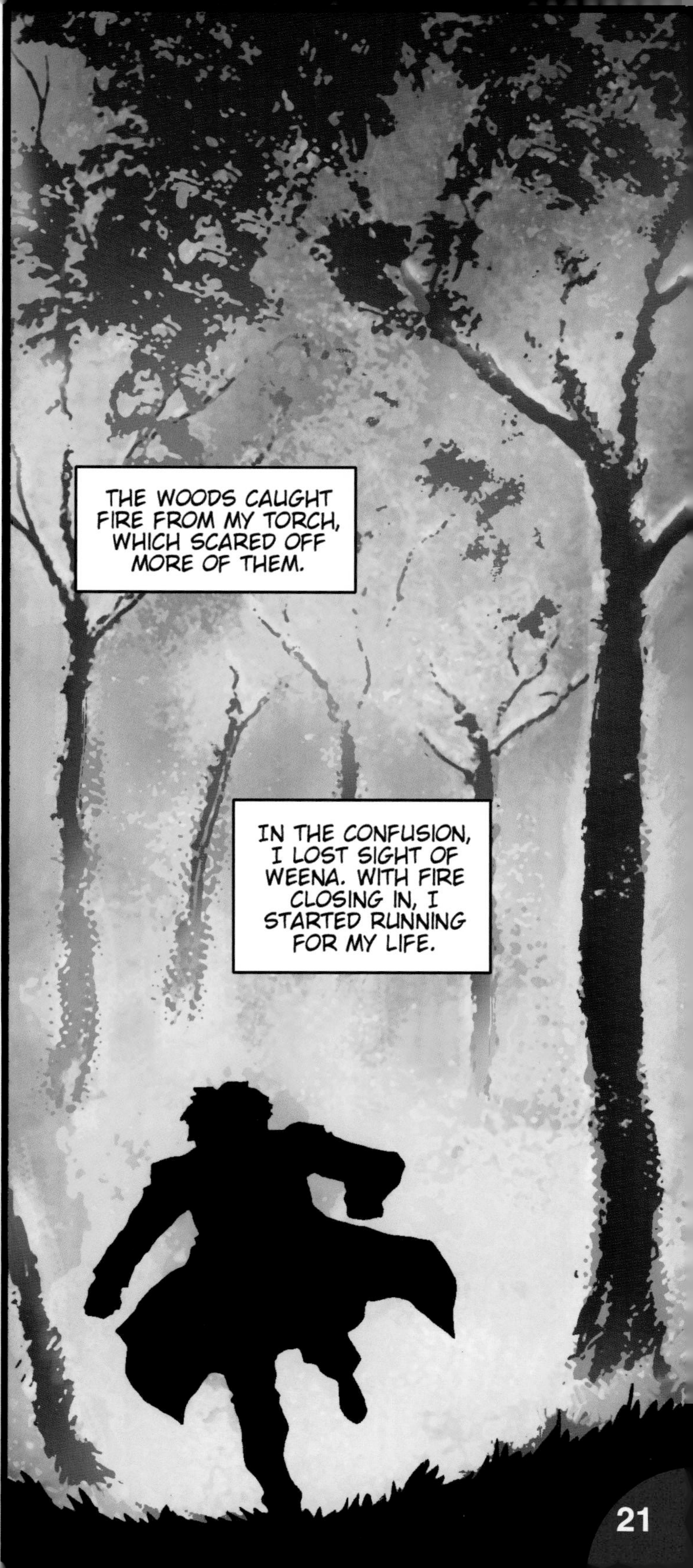
THE WOODS CAUGHT FIRE FROM MY TORCH, WHICH SCARED OFF MORE OF THEM.
IN THE CONFUSION, I LOST SIGHT OF WEENA. WITH FIRE CLOSING IN, I STARTED RUNNING FOR MY LIFE.

Chapter 5 Escaping into the Future

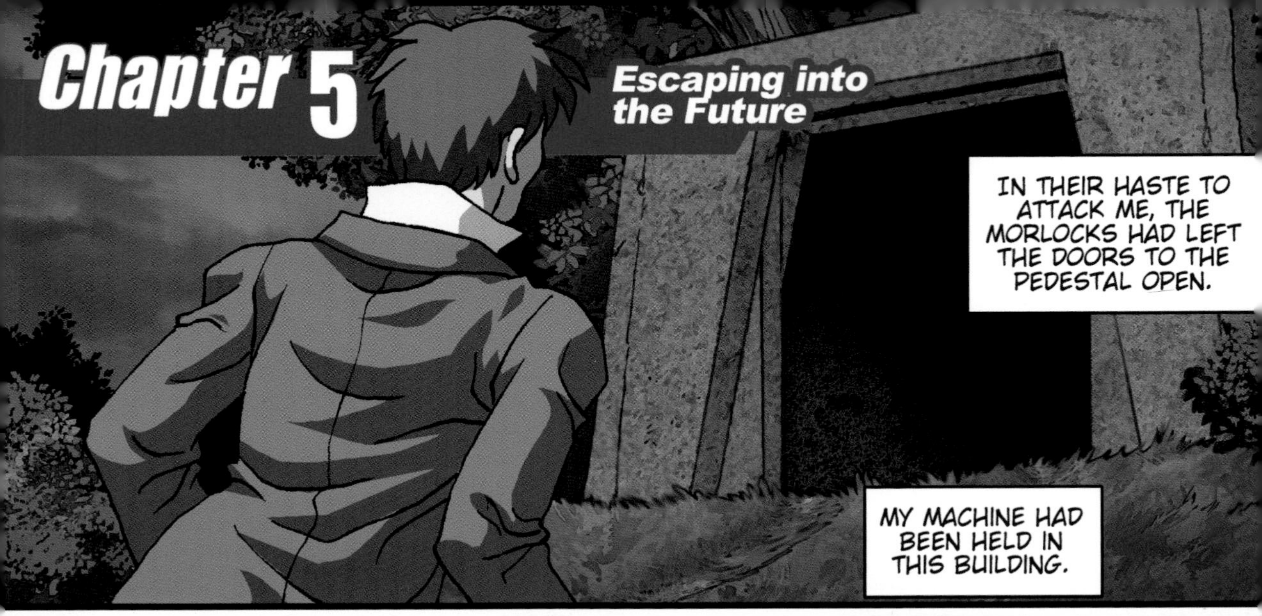
IN THEIR HASTE TO ATTACK ME, THE MORLOCKS HAD LEFT THE DOORS TO THE PEDESTAL OPEN.
MY MACHINE HAD BEEN HELD IN THIS BUILDING.

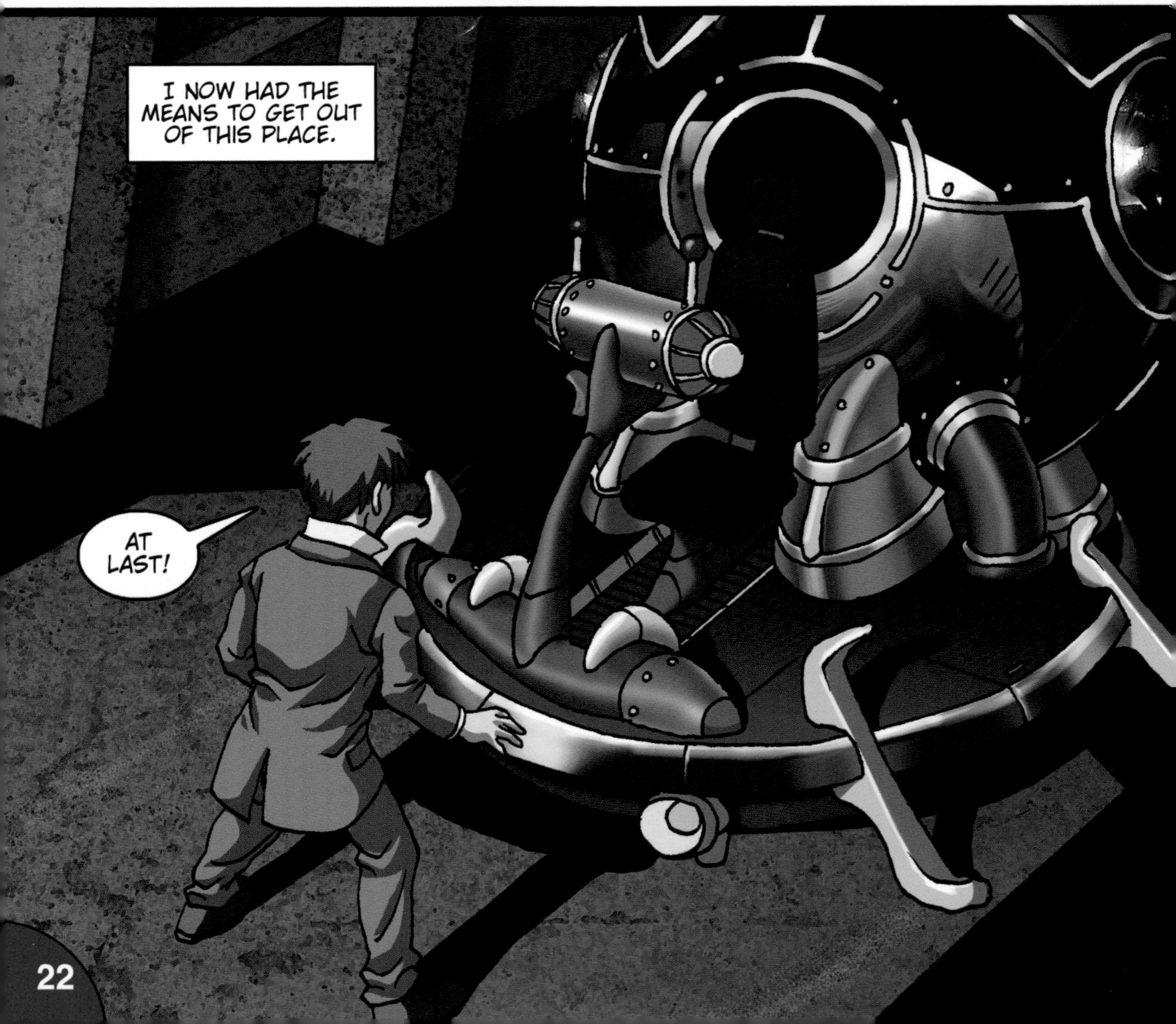
I NOW HAD THE MEANS TO GET OUT OF THIS PLACE.
AT LAST!

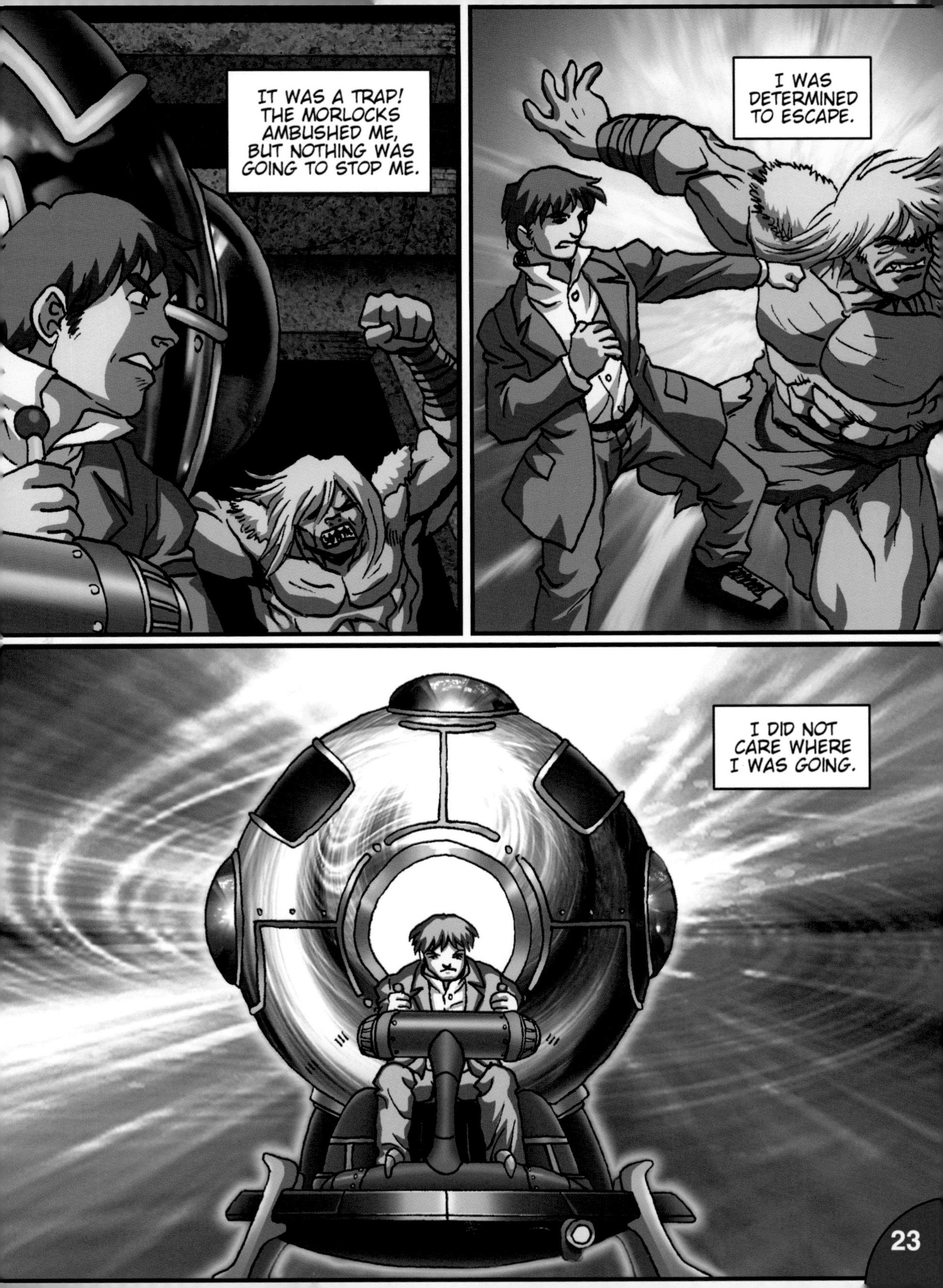
IT WAS A TRAP! THE MORLOCKS AMBUSHED ME, BUT NOTHING WAS GOING TO STOP ME.
I WAS DETERMINED TO ESCAPE.
I DID NOT CARE WHERE I WAS GOING.

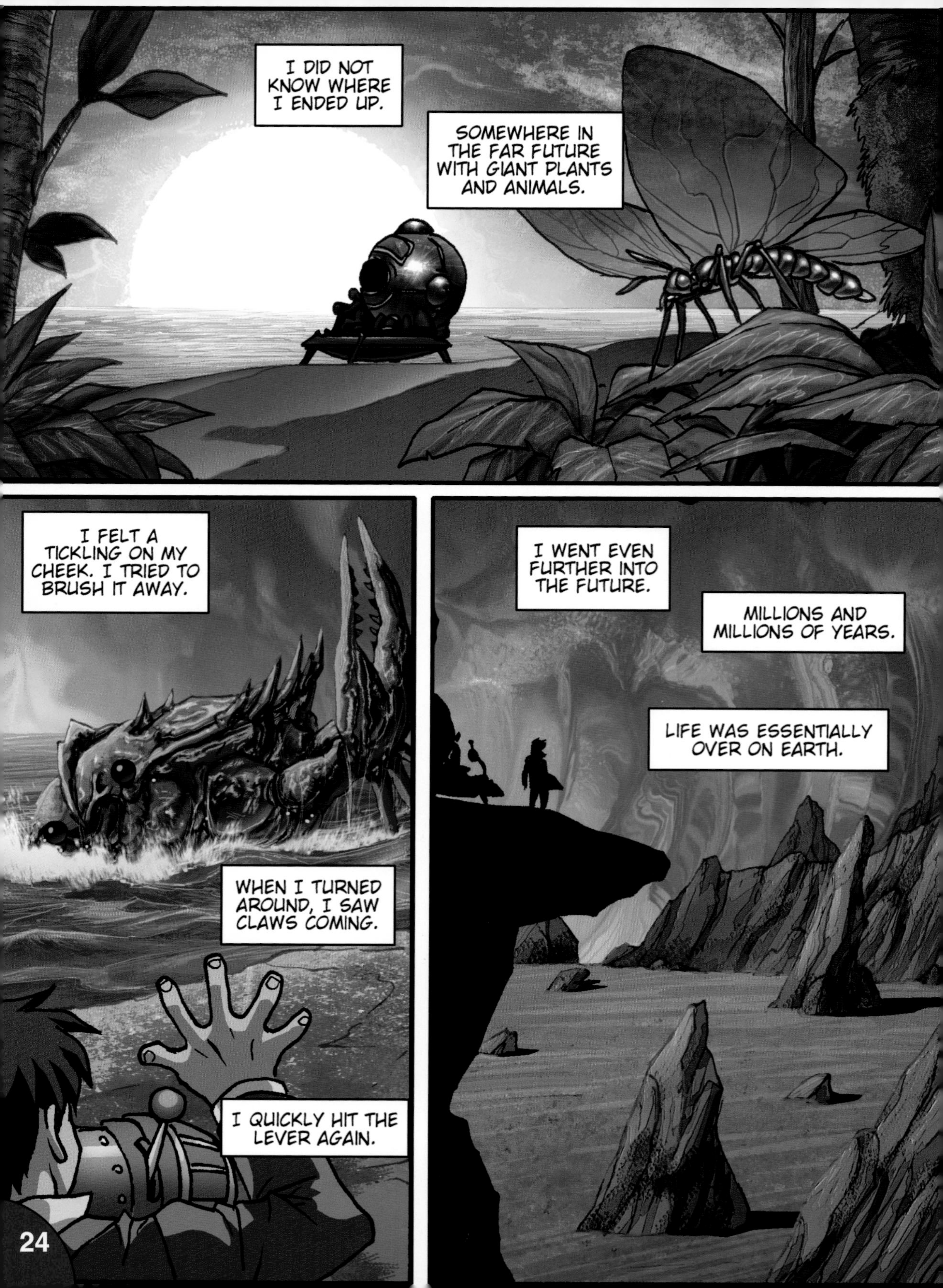
I DID NOT KNOW WHERE I ENDED UP.
SOMEWHERE IN THE FAR FUTURE WITH GIANT PLANTS AND ANIMALS.
I FELT A TICKLING ON MY CHEEK. I TRIED TO BRUSH IT AWAY.
WHEN I TURNED AROUND, I SAW CLAWS COMING.
I QUICKLY HIT THE LEVER AGAIN.
I WENT EVEN FURTHER INTO THE FUTURE.
MILLIONS AND MILLIONS OF YEARS.
LIFE WAS ESSENTIALLY OVER ON EARTH.

Chapter 6 The Voyage Home

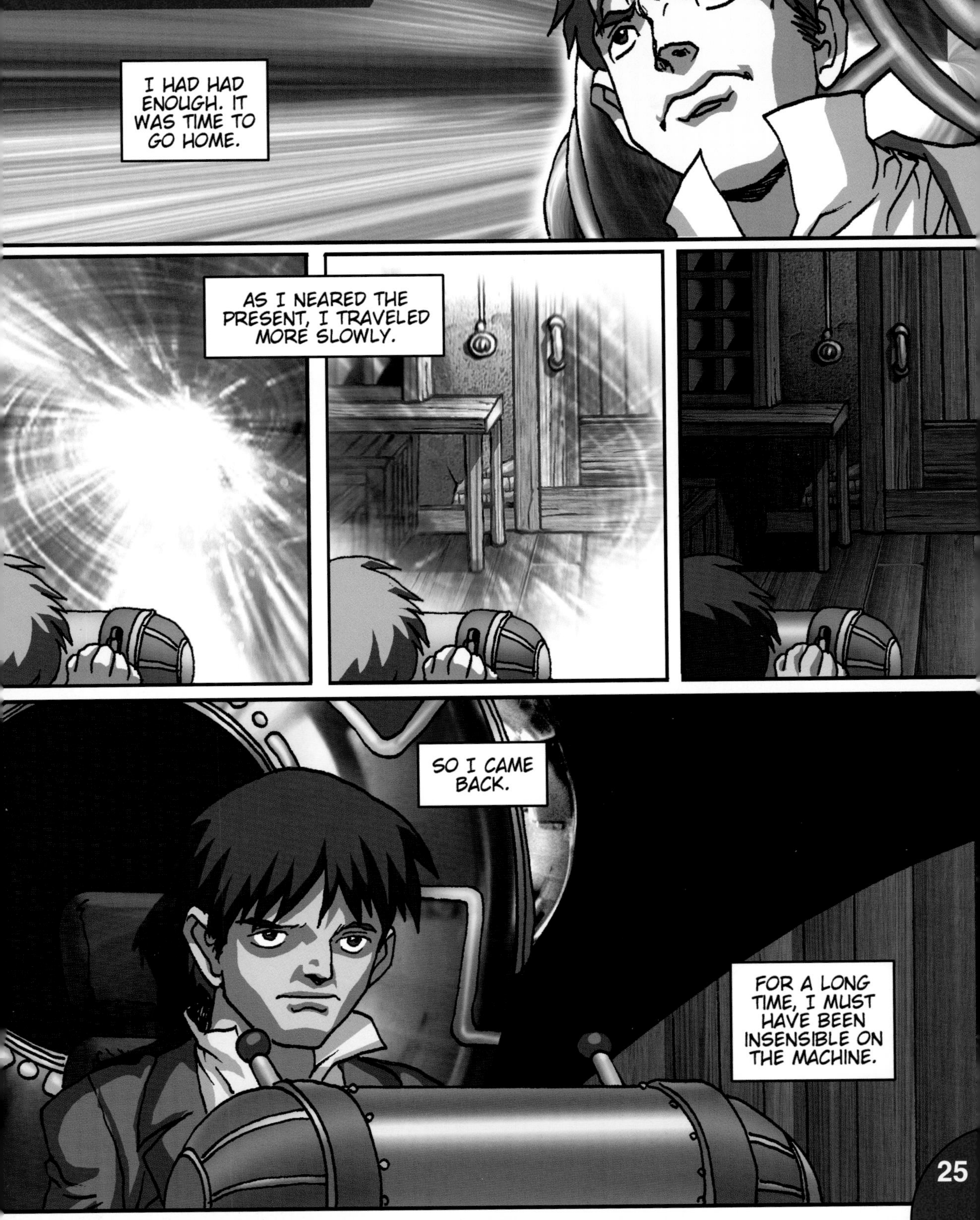

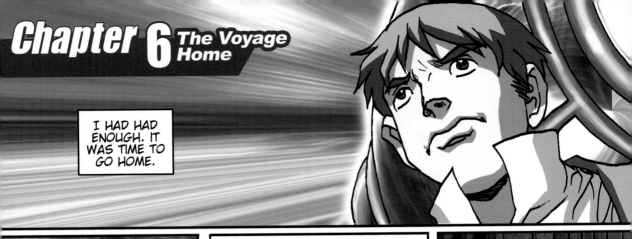

I HAD HAD ENOUGH. IT WAS TIME TO GO HOME.
AS I NEARED THE PRESENT, I TRAVELED MORE SLOWLY.
SO I CAME BACK.
FOR A LONG TIME, I MUST HAVE BEEN INSENSIBLE ON THE MACHINE.

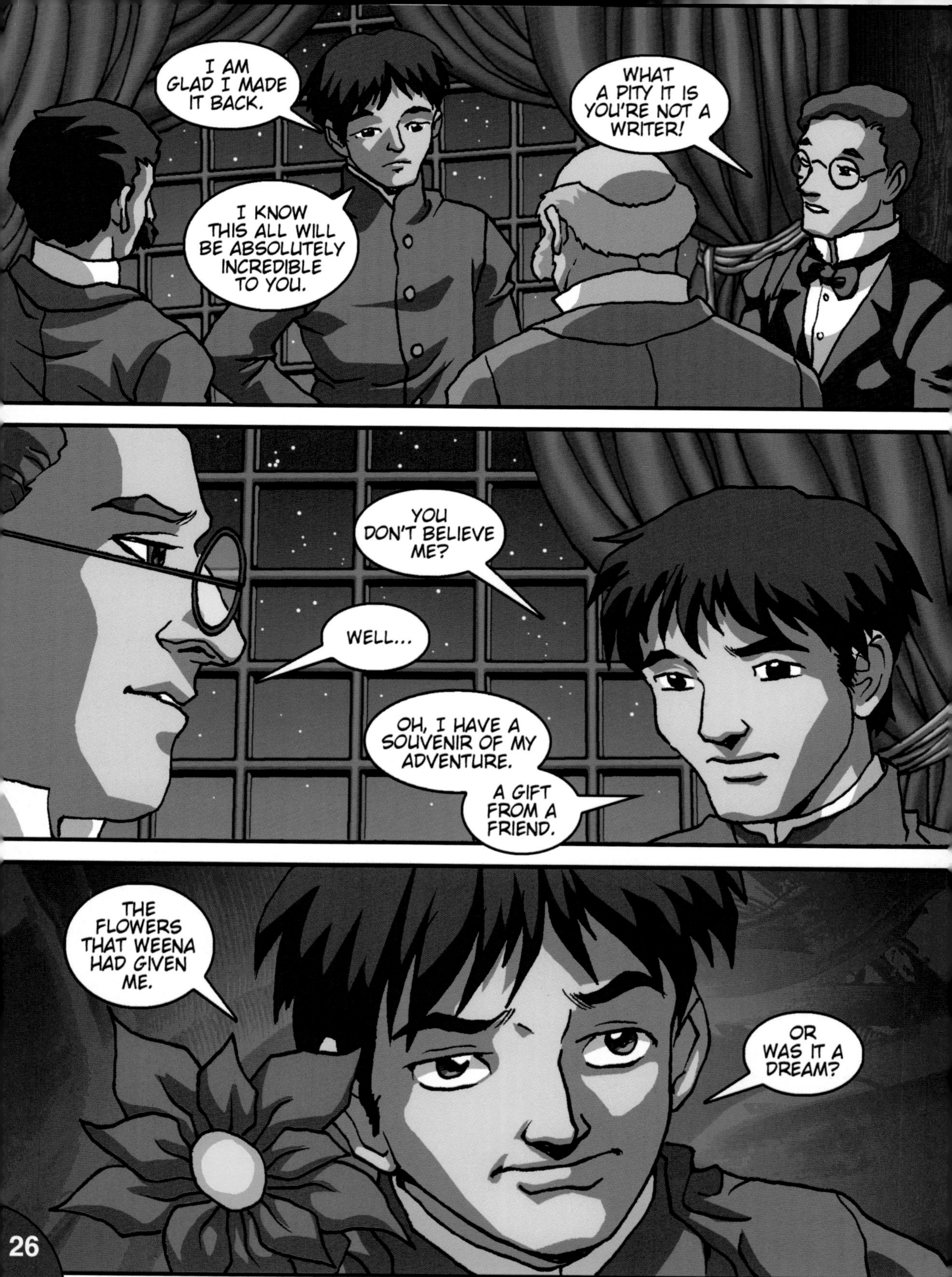
I AM GLAD I MADE IT BACK.
I KNOW THIS ALL WILL BE ABSOLUTELY INCREDIBLE TO YOU.
WHAT A PITY IT IS YOU'RE NOT A WRITER!
YOU DON'T BELIEVE ME?
WELL...
OH, I HAVE A SOUVENIR OF MY ADVENTURE.
A GIFT FROM A FRIEND.
THE FLOWERS THAT WEENA HAD GIVEN ME.
OR WAS IT A DREAM?

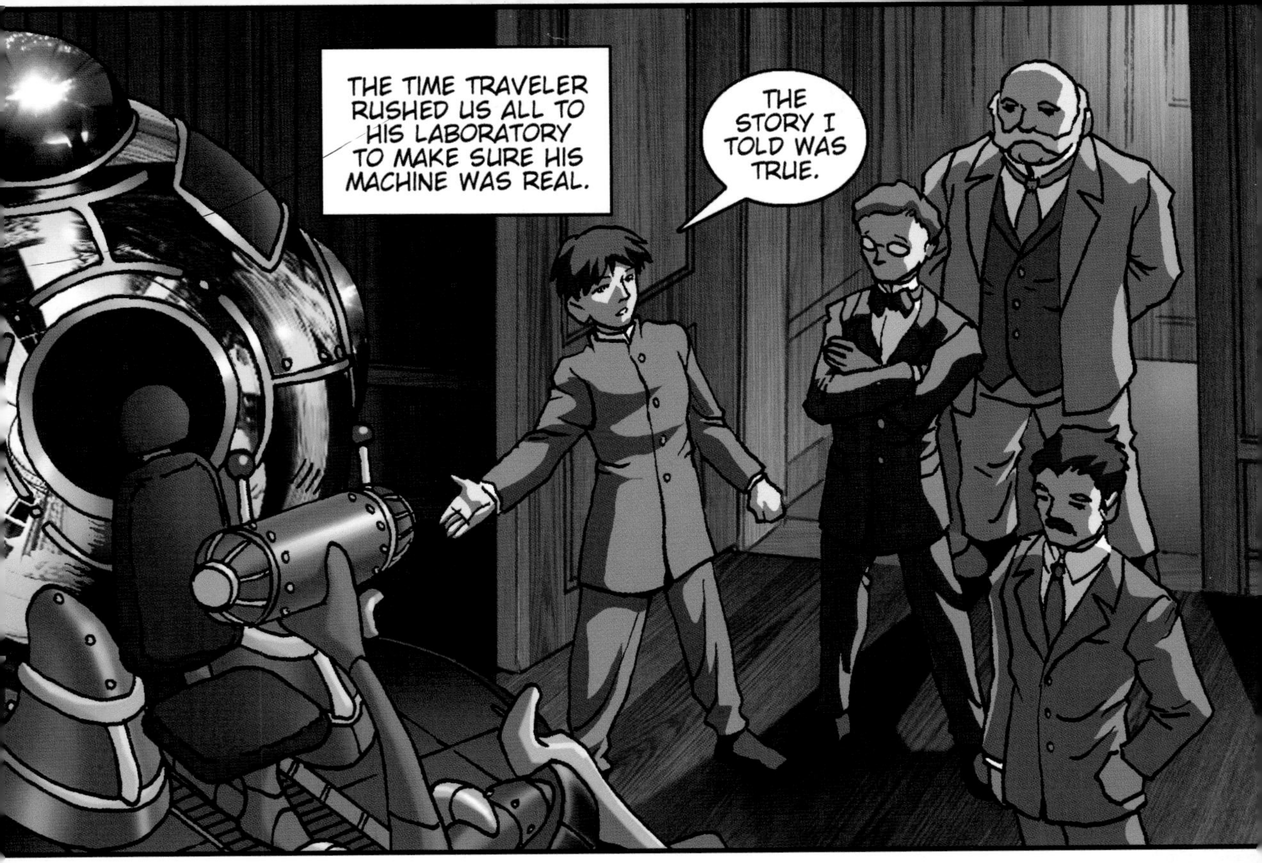
THE TIME TRAVELER RUSHED US ALL TO HIS LABORATORY TO MAKE SURE HIS MACHINE WAS REAL.
THE STORY I TOLD WAS TRUE.

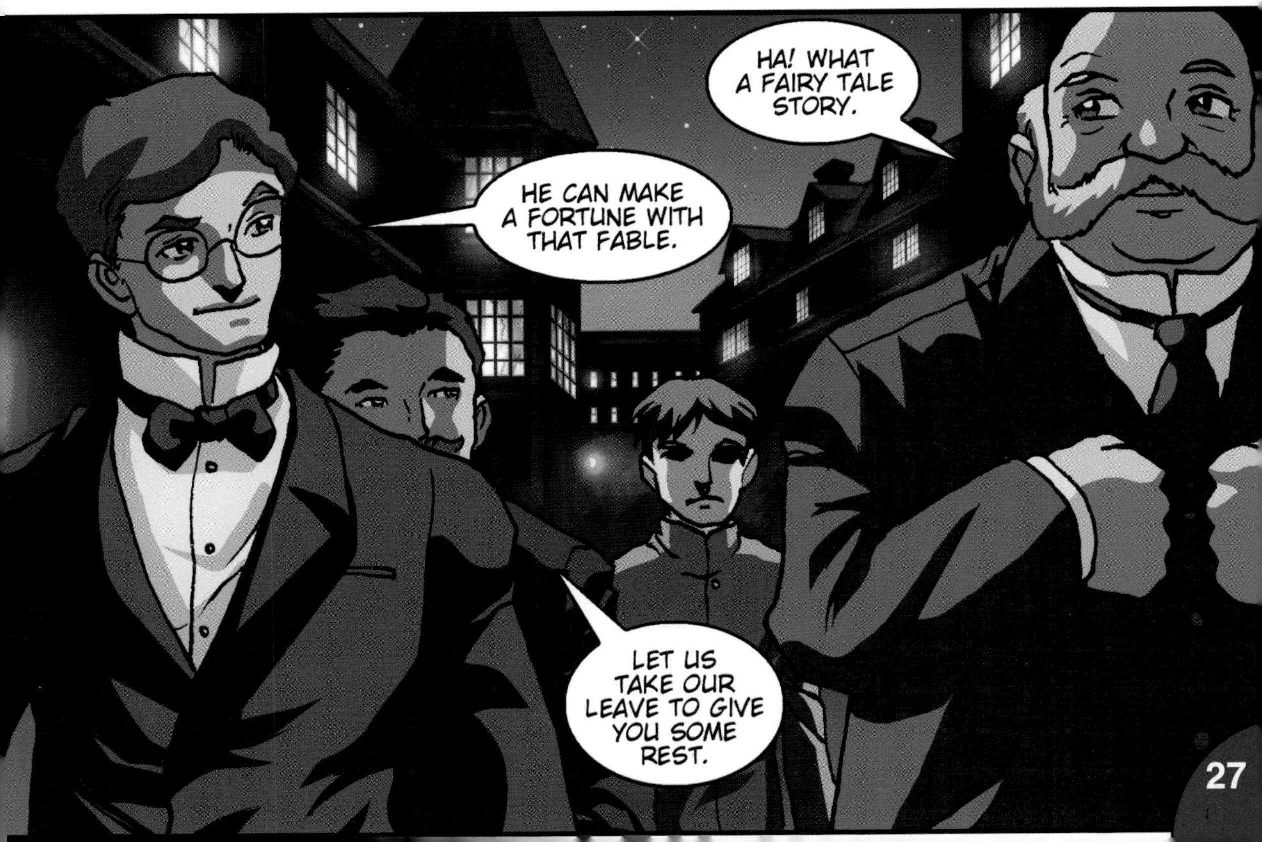
HA! WHAT A FAIRY TALE STORY.
HE CAN MAKE A FORTUNE WITH THAT FABLE.
LET US TAKE OUR LEAVE TO GIVE YOU SOME REST.

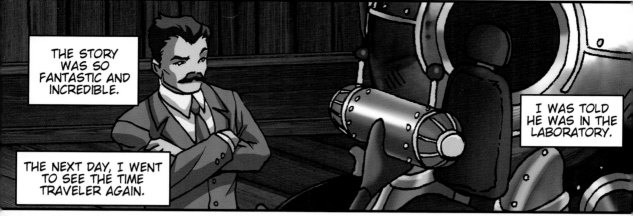

THE STORY WAS SO FANTASTIC AND INCREDIBLE.

I WAS TOLD HE WAS IN THE LABORATORY.

THE NEXT DAY, I WENT TO SEE THE TIME TRAVELER AGAIN.

I'M FRIGHTFULLY BUSY. I AM GOING AGAIN, AND THIS TIME I WILL BRING BACK PROOF.

IF YOU GIVE ME A HALF AN HOUR, I'LL TELL YOU OF MY TRAVELS.

I AGREED. THE TIME TRAVELER NODDED, AND I LEFT THE LAB.

THEN I REMEMBERED I HAD ANOTHER APPOINTMENT IN HALF AN HOUR.

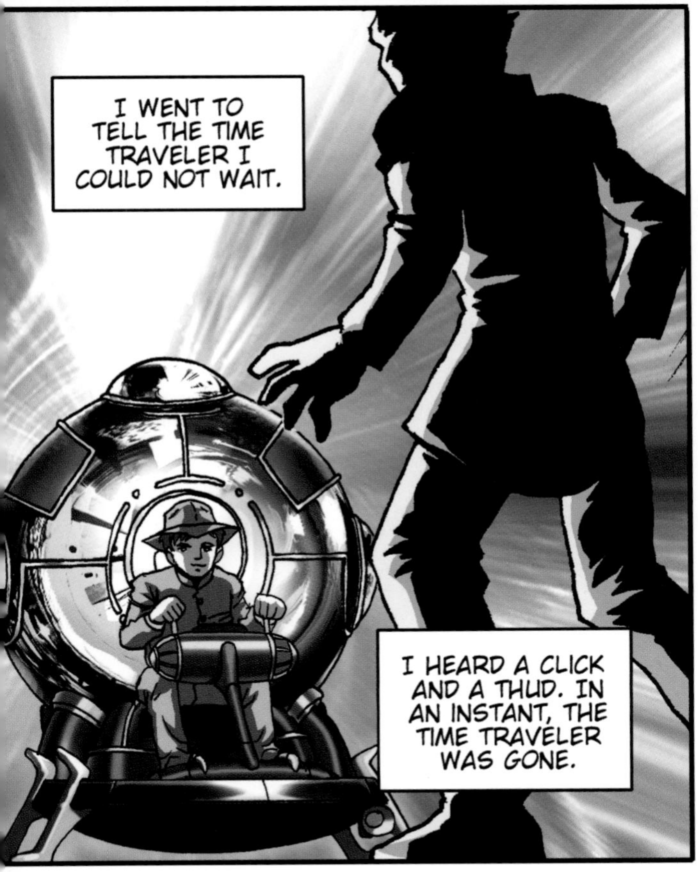
I WENT TO TELL THE TIME TRAVELER I COULD NOT WAIT.
I HEARD A CLICK AND A THUD. IN AN INSTANT, THE TIME TRAVELER WAS GONE.

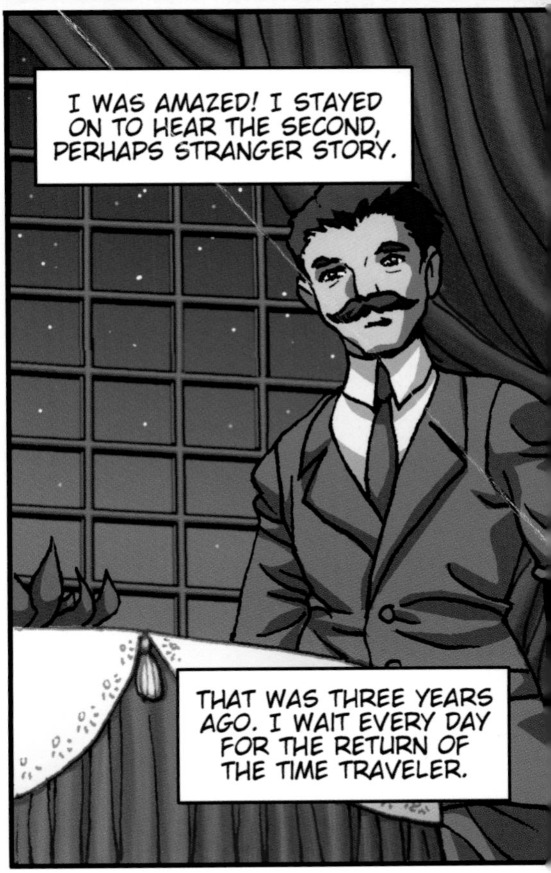
I WAS AMAZED! I STAYED ON TO HEAR THE SECOND, PERHAPS STRANGER STORY.
THAT WAS THREE YEARS AGO. I WAIT EVERY DAY FOR THE RETURN OF THE TIME TRAVELER.

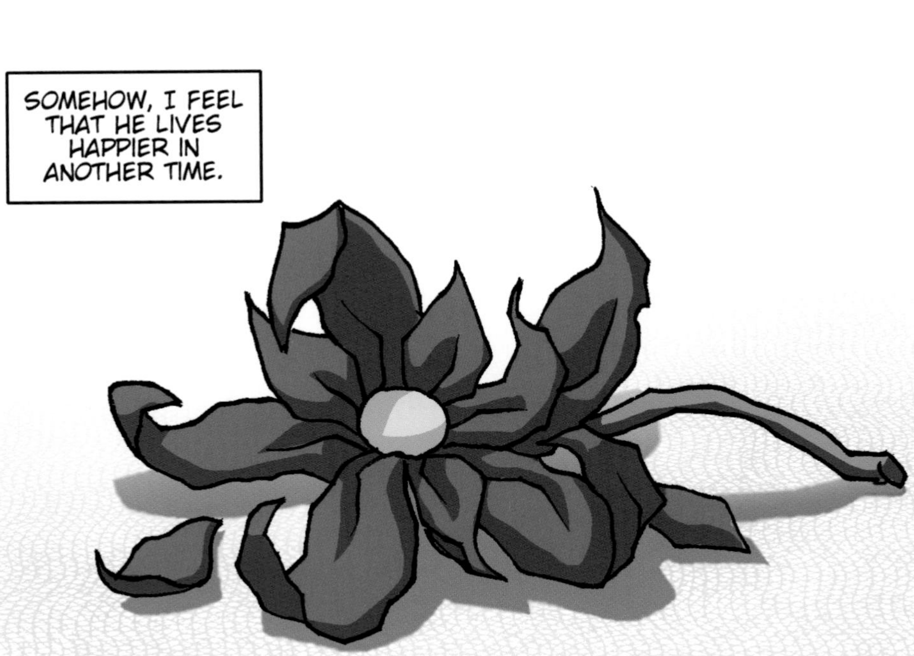
SOMEHOW, I FEEL THAT HE LIVES HAPPIER IN ANOTHER TIME.

About the Author

Herbert George Wells was born in Bromley, England, on September 21, 1866. His father was a shopkeeper and his mother was a housekeeper.

Wells attended Morley's School in Bromley, but did not get much of an education there. His real education came from reading on his own. At age 14, Wells was apprenticed to a drape maker but was soon dismissed. He then worked several jobs before becoming an aid in a grammar school.

At 18, he won a scholarship to the Royal College of Science. He graduated from London University in 1888 and began teaching. Wells had always been interested in science fiction. Soon, he began writing it himself.

Wells added creative touches to his stories. In 1895, Wells included the idea of time as the fourth dimension in his book *The Time Machine*. This concept was not discussed or accepted until 1905 when Albert Einstein published his paper on the relativity of time!

H.G. Wells died on August 13, 1946, in London. During his lifetime, he had written many successful nonfiction works. However, it is through his great science fiction works that he will be best remembered.

Additional Works

Additional Works by H.G. Wells

Textbook of Biology (1893)
The Time Machine (1895)
The Island of Doctor Moreau (1896)
The Invisible Man (1897)
The War of the Worlds (1898)
The First Men in the Moon (1901)
Mankind in the Making (1903)
Kipps (1905)
Tono-Bungay (1909)
Bealby (1915)
Mr. Britling Sees It Through (1916)
The Outline of History (1920)

About the Adapter

Joeming Dunn is both a general practice physician and the owner of one of the largest comic companies in Texas, Antarctic Press. A graduate of two Texas schools, Austin College in Sherman and the University of Texas Medical Branch in Galveston, he has currently settled in San Antonio.

Dr. Dunn has written or co-authored texts in both the medical and graphic novel fields. He met his wife, Teresa, in college, and they have two bright and lovely girls, Ashley and Camerin. Ashley has even helped some with his research for these Magic Wagon books.

Glossary

ambush – a surprise attack from a hidden position.

conscience – the part of a person's superego that sends commands.

contemplate – to consider with a lot of attention for a period of time.

dimension – one of four coordinates determining a position in space and time.

manipulate – to operate or control in a skillful manner.

Web Sites

To learn more about H.G. Wells, visit ABDO Publishing Company on the World Wide Web at **www.abdopublishing.com.** Web sites about Wells are featured on our Book Links page. These links are routinely monitored and updated to provide the most current information available.